T0146633

AFTER THAT AFTERNOON

HOW
RENTING
A MALE
ESCORT
CHANGED
MY LIFE
FOR THE
BETTER

Penelope Albert

authorHOUSE®

AuthorHouse™
1663 Liberty Drive
Bloomington, IN 47403
www.authorhouse.com
Phone: 1 (800) 839-8640

This is a work of fiction. All of the characters, names, incidents, organizations, and dialogue
in this novel are either the products of the author's imagination or are used fictitiously.

Published by AuthorHouse   08/31/2017

ISBN: 978-1-5462-0448-0 (sc)
ISBN: 978-1-5462-0446-6 (hc)
ISBN: 978-1-5462-0447-3 (e)

Library of Congress Control Number: 2017912618

Print information available on the last page.

Any people depicted in stock imagery provided by Thinkstock are models,
and such images are being used for illustrative purposes only.
Certain stock imagery © Thinkstock.

This book is printed on acid-free paper.

INTRODUCTION

S O, WHO IS this woman who decided that renting a male escort would be just a "good time?" Well, I am a 56-year old divorcee (been divorced for little over 18 years) and a Contract Administrator.

I have had only a couple of relationships during my lifetime. My marriage lasted 23 years and my last serious (well, it really was casual) relationship was for 14 years. I decided to dump that guy when I realized that he didn't want to go anywhere with me.

After that, I started going on vacations by myself (or sometimes my adult son would accompany me). I have visited Yosemite, Santa Barbara, San Jose, Santa Barbara (again), Newport, OR and Portland, OR. I love to drive so all my trips are within driving distance. Except my trip to Tucson.

Why did I want to go to Tucson? I found out that Roger Hodgson (formerly of Supertramp) was going to be in concert there. I was due for another vacation so I figured that it would be good place to go since I have never been there and I could see a concert.

I can't really say why I thought to myself, "Hmmm, some company would be nice on this trip. I wonder, should I rent myself a man? How do I go about doing that?"

I started my search on the internet. First, it was to research what it was like to rent a male escort. There is not a whole of information out there (seem like men really like to rent escorts – go figure) but I did find out that the women who did rent one were happy with the experience. It was an exhilarating time and an ego booster. That gave me a little more courage to do even more research.

Next it was, "How do I find a male escort?" Again, the internet was very helpful. I typed in "Male Escorts." I didn't know it but there a lot of male escorts for men. It seems that it is a big thing in the Gay community (that is speculation on my part). The things you can learn. So, I had to add at the end of my search "For Women."

There are a few agencies out there that cater to affluent women. Well, I am not affluent but if I was going to do it, I was not going to go cheap. I figured the more I spent, the more the escort would be classier, better looking and safe. Safety is always a consideration.

I found a website that looked very promising. It's like a yummy candy store. There are photos of all the men available and if you clicked on their photo, it would open their page and you can read all about them.

So many to choose from. There was one that I really liked but he was 25 years old. I really do have some self-respect and I couldn't see myself walking around town with a young man on my arm. It would be so obvious that I am a "cougar" so I looked for someone closer to my age.

And that is how I chose Andre. He was in his early 40's. Perfect. Brown Hair, a good height, a fantastic body (what a six-pack!) and such a charming smile. I could imagine him with me. After all, even though I was in my 50's, I could still pass for mid-forties so I wouldn't look ridiculous next to him. That is how I ended up on this journey.

In retrospect, this is one of the most embarrassing times of my life. I cannot stress enough how naïve I was. But something strange happened from this experience. I gained confidence in myself. I realized that I am enough to find a great man.

The heartache I endured is all in the past now so there is no ill will towards anyone. It was just a lesson learned and I am glad that I had to go through it so I could come out on the other side, a beautiful, feminine and sexy woman.

I thought it would be a good read (and it was therapeutic), so I wrote it all down. I mean, who else has been in this situation? Not anyone I have heard of.

Enjoy the story. Make sure you check out my footnotes (if you want to) as you go along. A lot of the growth I experienced is reflected in the footnotes. I have learned so much in a short amount of time.

Probably the best way to read this would be read it through one time, ignoring the footnotes. That way you get all the emotions unbroken. Then read it one more time, including the footnotes. I do apologize about so many of them but they really do tell how I feel about the whole experience now. They start in Chapter 3.

So, let's get this tale of my weekend started, shall we?

CHAPTER 1

ON MY WAY

I WOKE UP at 3:45 to the alarm, slicing through my dream of what was going to happen this weekend. It was a very nice dream. I would see the concert, meet the man, go to the zoo, have a meal and have a good time. And I would return home, having great memories. Ignorance is bliss.

The goal was to be out of the house by 4:00am which I did. I had prepared the night before. After all, it was going to be a weekend to remember. I had packed everything I could think of that I would need. I had comfortable shoes for the zoo. I had my camera to record the experience. I had a negligee for the rendezvous. Everything was ready to go so I was off to adventure the wonderful place called Tucson.

It was Saturday morning in December. When I looked up, the stars were twinkling, like they knew that this was the moment in my life I was waiting for. It was very quiet out as the sound of the garage door opening rippled through the neighborhood. I hoped no one would wake from the intrusion. It was so early. No cars were zipping down the road to take their owners to work. No one was walking their dogs so they wouldn't crap in the house. In fact, no one was in sight.

I made it to the airport in 20 minutes. This was a good sign. "Everything is going to go smoothly", I thought to myself. And then, of course, I missed the entrance to the terminal I needed (which I did last time I went to the airport) so I had to drive around the airport loop again. There's an extra 3-4 minutes that I hadn't expected to use. I finally found the parking lot and I made sure I put my parking ticket somewhere safe in my purse.

While I walked the path to the terminal, making sure to pay attention to where I was parked, I noticed that no one was around. My footsteps echoed as I strolled happily with my roll along luggage following me. The path I chose twisted and turned through the parking garage and I was hoping I would remember where I parked when I got back home.

I finally arrived at the terminal and the place was alive with activity. Bright lights, people moving about, cars stopping to unload strange people for flights to places unknown (to me). I no longer felt isolated in my thoughts.

I went to the airline desk area. They had machines (modern technology is great) to check in without waiting in line since all I had was carry-on luggage. I purposely made sure that I had luggage that I could carry on. Who wants to pay extra? Since it was just a weekend trip, I knew that my two bags would suffice. I used the self-serve machine and it was quick and easy. Boarding pass in hand, I went to the gate. Security was a breeze since it was so early. I didn't even have to take off my shoes (which I appreciated since I wasn't thrilled about walking around on a dirty floor with my clean socks).

The plane took off on scheduled and it was still dark outside. I was able to see the sunrise as it peeked through the early morning clouds by the Sierra-Nevada Mountains. It was beautiful. I should have taken a photo.

We flew down the valley passed by Mount Diablo, crossed over Highway 680, skimmed over San Jose and up the Peninsula. You can see all the man-made land from the air near SFO. The pilot landed the plane beautifully (it was a woman, I found out when I was debarking the plane).

I had a 2-hour layover from Sacramento in San Francisco Airport. For some reason, there were no direct flights to Tucson. I guess not a lot people want to go there from Sacramento.

I had arranged to meet my best friend Jasmine for breakfast since she lived in the Bay Area. I disembarked the plane and walked towards the front of the airport so I could meet her. There was art work on the way from the gate in glass cases. The usual stuff but there was this weird yarn thing (a messy ball of yarn in an odd shape, trying to pass for art) that I just had to get a picture of.

It took a while to find Jasmine (the airport was just so big) but we met up and I had half a muffin. Little did I know that it would be the start of me not eating very much food. We took a couple of selfies and I was off to security again to go to Tucson.

I was very excited about the weekend. The concert was that night. I had a great hotel room and I had a date the next day. Sigh.

It was a small plane. Smaller than the one from SMF to SFO. When we took off we made a U-turn from the airport to head south. I saw Santa Cruz, Monterey and I think Santa Maria before we headed inland. From there it was hard for me to tell where I was. There was a little turbulence on the descent. I hate turbulence. I felt like Jack from Lost, holding on to the armrest, like that would save me if the plane crashed. The Tucson Airport was small. Extremely small. We disembarked right on to the tarmac. I found the Car Rental Desk and got myself a 2017 Toyota Corolla with 316 miles on it. I was off to discover Tucson.

I figure since I had so much time to kill (I couldn't check into the hotel until 4pm), I stopped at the "Big Mart Store" to go to the bathroom. It looked like every other "Big Mart Store" but something was different about it. I think it was the lighting.

I needed to use the restroom. I hate using public restrooms. They are so dirty and full of germs. As it ended up, the one up front was closed for some reason so I had to walk to the back of the store to use the one there. Once I was done, I bought an 8-pack of water, a box of donuts, some chips and a puzzle book. I needed something for the hotel room to snack on and drink.

I drove around and it is such a desert (duh). It is so dry. If mankind hadn't built anything, there would be nothing but tumbleweeds and sand. I figure that I would drive down to the casino (where the concert was) to make sure I knew where it was before it was dark. It was quite a long way down the freeway. I found it and it looked like a casino (imagine that). There was this weird loop overpass thing that I had to drive over so I knew on the way to the concert I would use that as my marker. It was time for me to go back towards the hotel.

I went through a lot of small towns right next to each other. It was like Sacramento, where one town just runs right into the next with no break in the urban sprawl.

I stopped at one town since they had a Hell Taco and ate lunch. It was more expensive than the one at home. It was kind of awkward because after I went through the drive-thru, I parked in the adjacent parking lot and a guy pulled right in front of me (I mean, couldn't he park one space over?) and he was eating in his car (small SUV really). I bought a shredded chicken burrito but ate about half. I got a Cola, my favorite red, white and blue can soda.

I still had two hours to kill before I could check into the hotel. So, I was back on the highway going towards the hotel. I passed it by (nice hotel) and kept driving on the highway. It was more like a business route. It was ritzy in some areas with very large homes on both sides of the highway.

One thing I noticed about the area is the mountains come out of nowhere. Here we have foothills but there it's flatland and then mountains. They come straight up out of nowhere.

I drove around some more. I found another "Big Mart Store" (good thing they are plentiful) and went to the bathroom again. And as a side note, I do go to "Big Mart Store" for bathrooms because, honestly, they are clean. But by then, I was really bored so I called the hotel and asked them if they could get my room ready early. They said yes and they will call when it's available.

I was back near the airport again. Tucson is set up weird. Since it's in a diagonal valley, the streets zig-zag. So, I started zig-zagging back to the hotel area. I took some photos in an empty lot where all you could see is sand, tumbleweeds and small, dry plants. I was trying to get a photo of the natural environment.

The hotel finally called to let me know that the room was ready. I made a left at the wrong signal so I had to drive until I found a spot to make a U-turn. "I must remember that this is the wrong left," I thought for next time I drive back from that direction. I finally made it to the hotel.

Wow, I sure do know how to pick hotels. Since I started vacationing about 3 years ago, I only stay at higher end hotels. The thought of sleeping in a tacky motel did not appeal to me. Germs and bed bugs. Yuk.

It was the "H" Brand Hotel. It had beautiful fountains out front. They shot straight up into the air and landed in a man-made flat, rocky area with small river rocks. Since it was nearing Christmas, each fountain had either a red or green light illuminating them. The was a huge Wreath hanging over the entrance. Even though there was no snow (a small amount on the very tall mountains far away), it had a festive feel to it.

I stopped and talked to the valets to see where I should park. They pointed out the overnight lot (only $11.00 a night) and I parked the car. It was on the other side of the hotel so I unloaded my luggage from my car and went to the front desk to check in.

It was what I expected inside. When you enter the hotel, the registration desk was on the left. Straight ahead was a very large Christmas tree with wrapped presents under it and beyond that was glass doors that lead to a patio area. I could see that they had fire pits, tables and chairs that overlooked the golf course. Two restaurants, one on each side, were on your way out to the patio. The left side was more of a bar. If you made a left at the Christmas tree, the hallway lead to the elevators I needed.

I was on the third floor but the building was 5 floors. The two elevators on the right side only went up three floors but the one on the left side went up to the top. I took the elevator on the right side and I found my way to my room.

It was a very nice room. It had a separate sitting area that was two steps down (that I almost killed myself on once because I forgot about it).

The bathroom was great, with a separate tub and shower. Everything was brass and gold. Lots of towels, too.

I opened the blinds and looked around. It was a very pleasant view of the golf course (yes, I paid the big bucks to overlook it). I planned to walk the hotel grounds and golf course early Sunday morning and take photos, before I had to get ready to meet Andre.

CHAPTER 2

THE CONCERT

I TOOK A short nap because I was going to go to the concert and I usually go to bed early. I left around 6pm. The concert didn't start until 8pm. I am always early. There was a huge banner on the casino with Roger Hodgson on it. I parked the car among all the other cars and walked to the casino.

Man, casinos. I really do dislike them. They are noisy, smelly and artificial. I found the will call area and picked up my ticket. I was hoping my seat was decent. It looked ok on the seating chart. This was a spur of the moment vacation so I should have purchased my ticket earlier.

Now, I was kind of hungry (since I hadn't eaten since Hell Taco) and they had crappy food in the casino unless you wanted to go to the buffet, which is a waste of money for me. I don't eat enough food to pay $34.99 for a meal, especially a buffet. There was an Asian food place in a small food court so I ordered chicken fried rice. I figured it couldn't be that bad. It was the worst fried rice I've ever had. It was over saturated with soy sauce. Moderation, baby. I ate some of the chicken out of it and threw the rest away.

There was still a little time before the concert began and since I hate being in the casino (I don't smoke so the cigarette smell was so overpowering), I sat outside on a ledge and watched the people going in and out and the casino's valet service. It was a little chilly out but it was better than being inside. Snow is better than being in a casino.

Finally, it was close to the time for the concert to start so I went back in and found my seat. The seat wasn't in a bad location. It was off to the left but I knew that Roger wouldn't be that far away when he was at the keyboards. There was one guy who sat down a couple of seats to the left of me who was disappointed in his seats. So, I pointed out to him, "Be optimistic, the keyboards are right there. We will be close."

Nothing really went on until the concert started. I know, boring for a story but I could explain how people were moving to their seats and that isn't interesting either. So, I patiently waited and watched (people moving to their seats – lol).

It was time. They walked onto the stage! It was great seeing Roger and his band. The sound was amazingly good. And my seats had a great view of him when he was at the keyboards. But when he went to the Grand Piano, his back was to me. They had "the requisite big screen" and a couple of times I watched that when he wasn't facing me.

His band was so talented. Roger was super talented. He sang, played the keyboards, the Grand Piano and Acoustic Guitar (of course, not all at once). When they got into an instrumental jam, that is where they all shined. It was great! The other keyboardist was amazing. I had never seen anyone move their fingers so fast and not miss a key stroke. I have it on film (well, digital, which is what most recording is done on now).

And speaking of recording, I killed the battery on my phone! I have never done that. Ever. I did check the charge level before I left the hotel room and it was at 58%. I thought, "That's plenty. I won't be using it much, if at all." Ha!!!!! Little did I know that they didn't care if you filmed the concert so I started filming and filming and filming. I got some great footage. Man, if I would have known, I would have brought my good camera. But the memories are still recorded so I am pleased with that.

And, the concert was over. It seemed short. I think that because most of the time I was filming, and that took my concentration off the performance. It was two hours long though. I looked at my phone and knew what time it started. He played most of his hits (but not my favorite song which is "Even in the Quietest Moments").

Side Note: I had forgotten how good the concert was until I played the videos when I got home. It was excellent. Not always perfect singing but the musicians were outstanding. I really enjoyed myself that evening and was very happy having had that experience. It was a good choice.

When I left the casino, the temperature had dropped significantly outside. After all, it was the desert. I drove back to the hotel. The $11.00 lot was full so I drove to the valet area. I asked them, "What should I do?" They said that they would valet it for the cheap price. Yay! I got out of the car and gave them the keys. On another side note, the valets were super, nice people. I liked them a lot. Mostly early 20's Latinos.

Since it was a Saturday night, the Restaurant/Bar was alive with people and music. So different from when I checked in. It was raucous and it seem like a fun place to party.

I went up to my room and turned on the TV to wind down for

the evening. "The Starving Competitions" was on TV. A perfect movie to go to sleep to.

After all, it was going to be a big day. I watch a little and then I went to sleep, fantasizing about tomorrow.

CHAPTER 3

THE MAIN EVENT - MEETING THE MAN

S UNDAY MORNING. AHHHH, what a day it's going to be[1].
I woke up to the sun just rising in the distance. I grabbed
my camera and proceeded to take a few photos of the sunrise. It
was early because I always wake up early, no matter the day of the
week. I decided that I would just wear the clothing from the night
before since I knew I would be changing later that morning. I ate a
doughnut that I had bought at the "Big Mart Store" the previous day.

I wanted to make sure that I got photos of the hotel grounds. I
love taking photos. I am always trying to get a great shot. I happily
grabbed my camera again and headed to the elevator.

On the way out downstairs, in the hallway, I noticed the concierge
desk was open so I figured I could ask the lady behind the counter
about the zoo since I was planning to go there.[2] She said it was good
place to go and, by the way, they had discount tickets here, $3.00 off

---

[1] Man, if I only knew.

[2] I knew that I didn't want to spend 5 hours with this guy in the room so I had
planned something to do besides fool around.

each. Great!!! They charged it to my room. I liked that because then I could save what cash I had.

I then headed to the front desk. They smiled and greeted me a good morning. "Would it be ok if I went out to the golf course to take some photos?" I asked. One of the young men behind the desk replied, "No, you aren't supposed to be walking around there so I don't recommend it." Since I really don't care about arbitrary rules, I said, "Well, is anyone going to tackle me if I go out there anyway?" Both men laughed. I told them I was on my way there and they wished me another good morning.

I decided that I would cruise the hotel grounds first. There was a small man-made waterfall that ran under the road to the other side. Another attempt to get a great photo. There was a roundabout on the road and I was standing of the edge of the curb. I crouched down to get a photo of the waterfall without the road in the view. I stood up quickly and stumbled backwards into the street. And of course, there was a car driving there right as that happened. He stopped quickly and I smiled at him and waved. He seemed annoyed but I was happy so I just continued my trek to the golf course.

I arrived at the golf course. Everything is green (against the natural environment). I came across this putting green and I have never seen such green grass in my whole life. It was perfect. Every blade of grass was uniform. I bent down to look at it closely. I had to see perfection up close. I got a pretty good photo of it.[3]

I walked a little further down the golf cart road and came across another putting green area. There were two men on the putting green. One guy was talking up the other guy, like he was famous or

---

[3] I have been so distracted that I haven't even looked at the photos I took. I finally checked them out. I took some good photos!!!!

something. I wouldn't know but they were nice enough and answered the few questions I had about golf.

I came across this bridge for the golf carts to get to the other side of this man-made ravine that was in the middle of the golf course. There was a concrete ditch at the very center of the ravine. Luckily, it wasn't that wide so it didn't ruin the golf course view too much. I thought that was strange (the ravine, not the bridge). I did get some excellent photos while I was there.

Eventually, I did run across some guy who told me I had to leave the golf course. So, I did. It was about time I got ready anyway. I excitingly went back to the hotel and to the room.

"Oh Boy!!" I thought, "This is what I was waiting for". I was going to meet Andre (his stage name, I found out later).

I did everything to be attractive. I shaved and trimmed, you know where. I got in the bathtub and shaved my legs. That was nice. I don't get to do that at home. I had washed my hair the night before (I forgot about that). I put it up like I normally do (half up, half down). I brushed my teeth, flossed and put on some makeup. I normally don't wear makeup. I am a natural beauty.

I put on my nice, girly bra and panties that I had bought for the occasion. I put on socks, blue jeans, boots, my favorite t-shirt (Dragonball Z Vegeta – yes, I am a geek) and a light sweater. Oh, a little perfume, too. I wanted to smell good.[4] After all, we were going to be up close and personal. Nothing like a guaranteed good time. He was a sure thing.[5]

I went downstairs around noon and waited by the fire pits on

---

[4] Shortly after the event, I didn't even want to smell the perfume because it reminded me of him. It's fine now.

[5] Paying for it sure did help.

the patio while I played solitaire on my phone. Since I was nervous, I tried to call my sister to kill time but she didn't answer.

My phone beeped. Leonardo[6] texted me and told me that Andre couldn't find me. He even checked at the front desk. I told him that I am out back, like I said I would be. So, he told me that he would check again and text me back. When he texted me back, he told me that he found out that Andre was dropped off at the hotel next door and he would be over shortly. Since I knew he would be here before long, I went ahead and headed towards the valet areas. After a few minutes, he showed up.

And there he was, the guy I paid to put me through all this – lol - but not really.[7] As he approached, I noticed that he had a small suitcase rolling behind him. "I wonder what's in there?" I thought. As he got closer, I could tell that he looked just like his photos.[8] Man, was he good looking and what a smile. I really like(d) his smile.

I was nervous so, of course, I was doing most of the talking. I don't know about what. I know that we went back up to the room and we had hot, wild sex (ummm, too soon – lol – hahahahaha)[9].

Nah. We went up to the room so he could put on different clothes (that's what was in the suitcase) and I changed out of my boots to my tennis shoes. I told him that I thought we could go to the zoo and he said ok. He would have said ok to anywhere or anything.[10]

We headed back downstairs and he commented on how nice the Christmas Tree was in the lobby. We had to wait for the valets to

---

[6] The gentleman who arranged the meeting.

[7] Lots of money, too. You know what they say about a fool and his (or hers) money…

[8] I was glad that the photos were accurate. I did use a high-class agency so I was getting a high-quality man.

[9] I wish that was the truth. It would have been easier, I think. Maybe.

[10] It was his job to do so.

get the car because it was still in the valet area from overnight. We hopped in (oh, I usually tipped the valets $5.00) and we were off to the zoo. (weeks later addition – I remember that he asked if I wanted him to wear a hat or not[11] and I told him "Whatever you want is fine". He wore the hat).

As I began driving, he asked me if I knew where I was going. I told him "Kind of. I remember what the street name is and I know to make a left. I just don't know how far down the road it is." I told him that I try to use my memory for stuff, instead of an electronic device. We talked shortly about the dependence of electronics.

As I was driving, I was beginning to doubt where I was going. It seemed way down the highway. Then I told him about Nathan, my son, and how on our vacation earlier in the year, he would remind me to look for signs. And there it was, a sign,[12] pointing straight ahead to get to the zoo. It's a wonderful thing (signs). The street came up and another sign pointed the way, so I turned left. It didn't look like the right area but what did I know? I had never been there before so I just kept driving. After all, the signs wouldn't be wrong.[13]

I drove down that street talking about how old I am and that I can't imagine ever getting old and that when I do die, I hope I just drop dead. I think at that point I asked if he believed in God and he gave a positive answer on that. By then, I was wondering if I had gone the right way and, lo and behold!!! Another sign. The zoo was right ahead. I parked and we got out of the car.

It was unusually warm for December but it was the desert. I took my sweater off and tossed it in the back seat. We walked up to the

---

[11] He really was a gentleman.

[12] It should have said "Buyer Beware!!!!"

[13] I should have been paying attention to all the "signs."

ticket booth and the lady told me to wait (she was helping someone else). I wasn't sure what I was supposed to do since I had the tickets already. I waited for the guy in front of me and then I handed her the tickets and we were in.

The first thing we did was buy Andre a drink. I got a bottled water. I was looking at the map because there was a short hiking trail to go on but the park was all turned around. The map didn't make any sense. A guide tried to give us directions but that didn't help so we kind of just went to the right (whatever way it was).

Disclaimer: I know his real name now and I just feel weird calling him Andre in the story (even though, at that time, that is what I thought his name was). [14]

By the way, I am an idiot, but you will see. Way down in this story.

The first thing we came across was this model train scenery they had. It was very large (kind of like something else – I apologize. I couldn't help myself). I filmed a short video there. When I reviewed that video later, I swung by him and you can see him in a blur for a second.[15]

We walked some more and saw some small desert cats, a couple of rusted, steel lion statues and then this bull with extremely long horns.

We approached the giraffes and the place where you can feed

---

[14] I had to change the name to protect the "not so innocent". You bet on the original draft, it has the right name. So, all the time I was with him, I was calling him the wrong name but it was his "stage" name. The rest of the story, I had his real name since he told me.

[15] I have no photos of him except his "agency" one. I didn't know at the time what was going to happen. How it would change me.

them. Andre asked if I wanted to feed the giraffes and he would film me and I said sure. I handed him the camera.[16]

He started filming. "Say Hello!" he said. I waved and made a goofy face. "This was fun." I thought.[17]

The lady who was running the place asked, "So, who is feeding the giraffes?" I replied, "I am feeding." She smiled and said "You are feeding. Good girl. It's all about having fun."

I paid her the $5.00 for 3 carrot sticks and I approached the giraffe that was at the fence. The zoo had it worked out that the giraffes were in a gulley so they were ground level to us short humans. I grabbed one of the carrot sticks and held it out for the giraffe. I laughed out loud when he stuck out his tongue. Did you know that giraffes have extremely long tongues? Well, I might have been aware of that a long time ago but it really caught me off guard. I approached the giraffe, holding out the carrot and he grabbed it. I felt a little bit of his teeth. That was freaky.

The lady who worked the area had a suggestion. "Okay, a fun thing to do with him is to just to do this" and she proceeded to go up to the giraffe and feed him but with her back to the giraffe and holding the food up towards her head. Imagine putting earrings on, that motion. She further explained "That way, you get both of your faces. But look at the camera". I said, "Oh, okay. Ready, Andre?"

Andre said "Wow, say hello!! You got a new friend."[18] I fed him the two carrots and looked up over my shoulder and said, "He's

---

[16] This is exactly what happened because I reference my video.

[17] At that moment, I really was enjoying myself.

[18] He had a very nice voice. I have the video as a remembrance even though I don't see him.

huge!!!" And he was.[19] Even though the giraffe was in the gulley, he still towered over me.

Andre asked the giraffe, "What's up. Buddy?"[20] The giraffe started to walk away. Andre spoke for the giraffe, "Unless you give me more food…" and I finished the statement "I have no interest in you at all." The zoo lady chimed in, "It's all about the food." I agreed with her and said, "Just like any animal, actually."

Andre asked the giraffe, "Hi, how are you?" The zookeeper held a carrot stick far away from the giraffe and we cheered him on. "Com'on you can do it. Reach!!!" And he stuck out his incredibly long tongue and ate the carrot. Andre said, "All Right. We are off to the next adventure." He turned off the camera and we moved on. That was a nice memory.[21]

After that, we walked a little further and I filmed the giraffes again, walking. They had a large enclosure to hang out in. We talked about God and his sense of humor. Andre asked if the giraffe runs and I said, "I don't know, I have never seen one run." I have since looked it up and they can run up to 31mph!

We walked around more and looked at the other animals. There was a petting zoo there that we went to.

He did tell me that he was an open book so I could ask him anything, so I did. I don't remember all the questions that I asked (not that there were that many but I can tell you what I remember about what I found out). He was upset that the website I found him on wasn't updated and that the photos were old.

---

[19] Talking about the giraffe.

[20] Andre was a nice guy, I believe that he was just confused.

[21] There were some good times.

This is killing me, writing this, but here we go.[22] I am just getting emotional because I am getting to where I am getting to know him and why I will remember him. And why I miss him.[23] This is stupid. It's supposed to be a journal, not a cry-fest. Ok, onward with the story!

We saw the cheetah. Pretty cat. We looked for the bighorn sheep which had this whole mountain side to themselves but they were nowhere in sight.

At some point of time, we walked with his arm over my shoulder and I had my hand around his back/waist. It was nice. He had a very nice body. More than I would get in real life (but you never know what will happen in the future).

I think it was about 45 minutes in, he wanted to find a restroom so we did. It was near the exit and I told him that I was done with the zoo. He asked if I was sure and I said "Yes, let's get some food. There are a couple of restaurants at the hotel." He agreed.

So, it was back to the hotel. And, of course, I tried to make a left turn at the same place I did the day before. It looks just like the entrance of the hotel I was staying in (so much for taking note of the wrong turn). I told him I made the same mistake yesterday.

I just valeted the car because I didn't want to deal with it. It's getting close to time. Oh, boy.[24]

We walk into the hotel and the restaurant was closed (too early) so we went across the hallway to the bar and ask them if they served

---

[22] We are heading towards the emotional stuff. It's not fun but it is authentic.

[23] It's so much later now that it's hard for me to remember the feelings that I felt. But since I wrote them down, they were real at the time.

[24] I was so excited. I hadn't been with a man for 3 years.

food. They said yes and we went outside to the patio to wait for them to take our order since it was nice weather.

We talk about a lot of things. He tells me that he is starting up a business online and asks me about taxes and being online. At first, I misunderstood that he was asking a question. I ended up telling him that no matter what, the government will get their cut.

He mentions that he has an ex that he recently broke up with.

I tell him that my mom's birthday is tomorrow and he says that his son's birthday is tomorrow. Really? Really.[25]

I mention that I like to go to Santa Barbara for vacation and he tells me that he knows exactly where the hotel is that I normally stay at. He asks if I have ever been to the underground club there. I told him no and he mentioned that we should go there sometime. [26] He does that stand-up paddle thing I saw in the harbor (when I stay in Santa Barbara, I stay right on the harbor) and I told him I had seen people doing that.

I was telling him where I invested my stocks and why. I mentioned I invested in a cigarette manufacturer[27] so marijuana got brought up.[28] I found out that he smoked, too and he was surprised that I did. He asked if I had any and I said, "No, I didn't want to take it on the plane." He said that no one would know. He said that if he knew he would have brought some. I believe he said that he liked Indica because Sativa puts him to sleep.

I told him that I like to go to comic cons and that I like to dress

---

[25] It was true because it was verified to me on social media.

[26] I was foolish enough to think he meant that.

[27] I invested in them because when marijuana becomes legal, I will be ahead of the game because I figure that they are going to diverse and start growing that crop. Cigarettes are on the decline.

[28] I have quit smoking since then. I don't need it anymore.

up. He asked me with fascination, "So, you like to dress up?" I said yeah. So, I get out my phone and show him a photo of me in costume but for some reason I also showed him the one of me, my dad and Nathan. He said that Nathan was cute (at 2 years old, he was cute) so I showed him a photo of Nathan now. He commented on his facial hair but I don't remember what else he said.

I also showed him the view from the hotel in Newport, OR.[29] I told him I love the ocean and he said he did, too[30].

See how well this is going? It's like amazing.[31]

We talked about death and how that I believe when we die, we wake right up. We both fear not existing. I talked to him about "time" and I find it fascinating that we are here now but time will go by and this will all be in the past. It's just memories now.

The food took forever to show up (probably 45 minutes but we were chatting and really didn't notice how long it took). He ordered wings, calamari and a burger. The food came out and I ate hardly anything. I did have a couple of wings and a couple of fries. His burger was kind of raw so they took that item off the bill. I remember that he wouldn't drink a beer because I don't drink, even though I offered to buy him one.[32]

He opened doors for me. He smiled at me. I was excited to be spending time with such a wonderful guy. He had good looks, was a gentleman and had a fantastic body.[33]

OK, we are getting to the part where you might want to stop

---

[29] This is where I went on vacation with my son earlier in the year.

[30] I recently realized through online dating that 95% of the population loves the ocean.

[31] The strong connection was there, I could feel it at the time.

[32] Since he was my escort, I paid for everything which I didn't mind.

[33] He was well versed in making a woman feel special. He was nice.

reading, if you don't want details of the encounter. I imagine though that is why you are reading this.[34] The previous stuff above is foreplay. We are about to get to the action. I will try to stay as classy as I can. But man, this is some good stuff.

You know, I don't think I will go into detail.[35] I will just have to remember it as is. But some highlights, listed in no particular order.

Him forgetting condoms and being so apologetic about it.[36] It's so sweet. We tried to have room service bring some to the room (oh, that was so funny when he called to asked[37]) but it took too long. I ended up getting dressed and going downstairs to buy some myself. And I left him in my room and didn't give any thought to it. In fact, I didn't even realize I did that until a few moments ago. I trusted him with my things.

Oh, wow.[38]

Taking a shower afterwards. He did ask to use my toothpaste.

Him giving me three sweet kisses goodbye[39]

Him saying that I was special and that he meant it (and I knew he did)[40]

Circumstances in life sucks a lot sometimes. He left and we tried

---

[34] I originally wrote this as a journal and I didn't want my son to read this accidently so I was giving him fair warning to stop reading.

[35] This story is about what happens after the encounter so I didn't want to turn it into a tawdry, romance novel. We only spent 5 ½ hours together but it was enough.

[36] Okay, so he's an escort and forgets condoms. Sorry, but he wasn't that together in his life.

[37] Him standing nude, talking on the phone.

[38] He was huge. I don't mean huge. I mean HUGE!!!! The biggest cock I have ever seen, even in porn.

[39] They were sweet, just quick kisses, no tongue.

[40] I really do think that at the time, it was real. I mean, why would he lie? For a repeat client? Who know?

to stay in contact but it didn't work out. I am still sad about it. I thought he was the most fantastic guy. The end.[41]

Not over yet. There is more pillow talk.

We were on the bed. I couldn't believe that he was here for me and I was all giddy about it. I told him so and he smiled.

I loved looking down at him. Us and our hair. Between the two of us, there was so much hair. I liked his hair. It was long, curly and soft. He asked me why don't I just bun it in the back. I told him that won't work. He said, "But your hair is longer than mine." He proceeded to show me with his hair.[42] I was straddling him while we were on the bed so I turned around and told him go ahead and try it with my hair. Then he understood. My hair is way too thick to do so.

We talked about his chest hair and that women usually like him clean shaven. I told him I like hair on a guy. He said that give him a month's notice before I see him again and he would grow it out for me (really, that was said)[43]. He said that he liked gray hair and I told him I dyed mine and that I hated it and am waiting for it to grow in.

Finding music that suited my mood was interesting. He suggested Maxwell so I tried that and that wasn't cutting it. I tried Hall and Oates. Mistake. And then I knew what I wanted. The Blues! Stevie Ray Vaughn! Now, I had a great soundtrack! We danced at one point (more near the end of the encounter). He said, "See? You can dance".

Us being so apologetic to each other because of the problem

---

[41] I actually thought, at that moment, that I wouldn't be writing any more. It ended up being so much more.

[42] His hair was thin so it was easy for him to do.

[43] It really did sound promising. I guess I was lonely or naïve or something. I just roll my eyes now.

(which was his really, BIG dick – it wouldn't go in without hurting so we never did "the deed"). That was sweet.

While we showered, I massaged his shoulders. I know that something was said that I was a great person (along those lines) and I started to say I try, but then I changed it to I am just me. He agreed. I am just me. Much later, I remembered that he did comment on the massage soap and that it was good soap.

The things I learned. What his real name was. That was nice of him to tell me.

He did give me his email and phone number.[44] I think that was, maybe, just for Uber. He told me that he had a DUI and that's why he needed an Uber ride. He asked me if I use Uber, and I replied, "No, why would I? I have a car."[45]

He looked nice when he was leaving. He had dressed in a nice pair of pants and a sports coat.

I am journaling this because I don't want to forget. It was a great experience and once time goes by, I can smile at it all.

But not now.[46]

Oh, I remember something else. When we got up to the room, I told him that I like to get dressed up but don't have much of an opportunity to do so right now in my life. So, I bought something special for the occasion. I asked him if he wanted to see me in it and he said yeah. I went to the bathroom and changed. I looked good. Of course, I bought something I looked good in. But I looked good.

And what he had for me. While I was changing in the bathroom,

---

[44] He really didn't have to. For future business?

[45] And a license.

[46] I love time. It's fascinating. Time changes always, and I knew in the back of my mind, this will pass.

he had changed into different briefs. I slowly peeled them off and gasped!!![47]

It was good times. My problem is that I want them to continue and logically, they can't. I am sad.

One more thing.....

When he was getting ready to leave (I asked him if it was a client and he told me, "No more clients"), he stood at the big mirror near the entryway and put on some makeup. He said that it was an old habit from when he modeled. Maybe he was a little insecure. [48]

We sent text messages after he left. I am going to record them here.

I now know why I got so hooked on him upon re-reading those. Beside the intense chemistry (which I don't feel with the man I am seeing now but he has other attributes that I really like, he treats me well and I like him a lot), I believed what he said (text) because I am an honest person and wouldn't lie about stuff like this. But as I learned, people can be deceiving. Especially if they think they can benefit from it.[49]

---

[47] I was shocked. No one should be THAT BIG. It really was useless but I am not a big person either so that didn't help.

[48] He might have just liked to wear makeup, too.

[49] Like a future paid visit from me.

CHAPTER 4

THE CRUSHING AFTERMATH

T HESE ARE THE text messages that were sent between us
after he departed the hotel room. So, without further ado,
here they are.[50]

That evening right after he left.

> Me: He's going to be there in a gold Lexus SUV
> And thanks for coming to visit me

> Him: Thx let me know when he calls you!
> Him: Of course you are an Amazing. Soul and spirit

> Me: He called[51]
> Oh, I didn't read that right haha
> You on your way?

> Him: Yes!

---

[50] They will be inserted at the proper time throughout this book. The same with
the emails. I didn't start journaling my feelings until I couldn't figure out what was
going on. It was all so confusing.

[51] The Uber ride that I paid for.

Thx so much

Me: Great had a really good time with you

Him: Same really special
Mean it

Me: Thanks Andre
I will see you again sometime soon

Monday, The next morning.
6:22am

Me: Good morning Andre. I have great memories of yesterday so thank you. Once I get home I will go ahead and add you to the "most popular social media"[52]

Me: And see I told you I get up early anyway

8:58am

Me: Just curious are you awake?

Him: Hi babe
Just woke
Loved being with y
U taught me a lot just being with y

---

[52] That never happened.

Me: The same. I really am looking forward to seeing you
again

Him: Same[53]

Me: We got along so well. It is so great.
I found out what's wrong with me
You know I would look it up[54]

Him: What?

Me: Actually, it's just the lack of estrogen
It affected my body more than I thought it would
That can be fixed for next time so that's good
But besides that, your company was great

Him: Ok

Me: The reason why I asked if you were awake earlier was
because I saw your hotel and I thought hey if you're
awake I could see you real quick. I am at the airport
now though
A funny story. I looked all over for the room for the
room key and could not find it at all. I was all packed
up ready to leave the room and I happened to glance
at the floor by the front door and there was the room
key on the floor. Haha.

Him: Haaaaa

---

[53] Why would he say that?

[54] I do not let anything go by if I don't understand it. I must know what is going on.

Him: That's crazy!!

 Me: Exactly
 Since I didn't find it till right before I left I spent the
 whole morning in the hotel room so I didn't have to
 tell the front desk that I lost the key.

Him: That's u boooo

Him: What about ur flight?

 Me: Well I'm sitting at the airport now I should be
 boarding in 10 minutes. I will let you know when I
 get on the ground in SFO
 You going to be heading home soon?

Him: Yes

Him: 1-ish
 Thx for everything Hun xoxoxo

 Me: Good for you. I'm looking forward to getting home.
 Same here. Sincerely, I am so glad I met you.
 Plane is delayed 45 minutes rats
 They just announced it

Him: Kk

 Me: Ok I will talk to you sometime in the very near future.
 have a safe trip home.

Him: Cocoa[55]

> Me: Finally made it to SFO. Now I 'm waiting for the plane to show up its not even here for my connecting flight
> Did you make it home?
> I am now in Sacramento

Him: No cry
I missed it[56]

> Me: Oh bummer. I should have drove you to the train station
> What was that the bus? Either way I should have drove you

Him: I'm so sad

> Me: I'm sorry to hear that. So, what are you going to do next?

Him: Never land

> Me: Never Land?
> Are you ok?

Him: No
To be honest

---

[55] Not sure what that was about. Maybe voice recognition messed up. I don't know.
[56] Another red flag. Or at least I should have realized how flakey he was but I believe everyone until I can't.

Him: But with u I was[57]

Love money security is all gone[58]

Me: Well sometimes it goes that way. Just got to keep chugging along and do the best you can with what you got

Things will work out for the best. They usually do if you are a good person. And I feel you're a good person[59]

It's not like I really have a great happy home life either

I just try to stay optimistic and do what I can

That's the best pep-talk I can give you. I just hate to see you down.[60]

Me: Here is a photo of me. So, smile. You can make it.

(I took a photo on my phone and sent it to him via text).

Him: Luv

Me: You know you could just get a traditional job for now to get you by

I know it's a Daily Grind. I do it every day. But I survived.

Every once in a while, I get something special like you

---

[57] Bullshit? Who knows? I seriously think he was a confused person at the time.

[58] Asking for money in a roundabout way.

[59] Was he a good person? He did mess with me but I don't think it was intentional. My naivete messed with me more, I think.

[60] I am a nice person and at that time I did care.

I am watching the movie Deadpool right now. Have you seen it?[61]

Tuesday 8:02 am

Me: Good morning. Am I texting you too much? If I am, I can stop.

First of all, I apologize for texting you so much. I had forgotten about the emotional Fallout of having sex with someone.[62] And it's not a bad thing. You know us women. So, if you don't want to contact me again just say it. And if I don't hear from you at all, I definitely know.

Him: No I'll call u![63]

Me: Oh, you're so sweet. I am running a big gambit of emotions though. I had forgotten about it.

Women and their emotions. What can you do? Haha.

Him: Xooxoxo

I'll call u when I have a few[64]

Me: I should let you know that I work Monday thru Friday 8:15 to 4:45 with lunch around 1 so you know

---

[61] And I should have realized that he was not interested in small talk.

[62] It's strange, I have had sex with a couple of guys since I got back and there was not this emotional fallout. I think it was just him.

[63] Lie number one on calling me. Did he intentionally do that? There is a lot I don't know since this is from my point of view.

[64] Redundant, I know but here is the second time.

Thanks for being such a great guy[65]

Him: Xooxox

Wednesday 6:58pm

Me: To text or not to text, that is the question

Him: How Hun

Me: Hi

Him: At gym how are u

Me: Honestly, I have all these emotions going around. It's crazy[66]
Voice recognition isn't what it's supposed to be
I am very happy you responded though
Maybe you can call me later?

Him: Tomorrow[67]

Me: Ok
Sounds great. Talk to you then.
Oh, and have a great weekend.

Him: Have stuff going on after gym xooxoxo
Nite

---

[65] Still living in the fantasy.

[66] I was crazy.

[67] Uh, huh.

Me: Goodnight

Thursday 11:08 pm

Me: Hi Andre. I am going to bed now. You must be busy.
Goodnight.[68]

Him: Honey I'm say upset
Please just listen I will
Give me a min
I need love and money right now[69]
God first[70]

Me: Okay. I know you are going through a tough time
right now. Unfortunately, I don't have a whole lot of
money. I made a special treat for myself to meet you.

Him: Kisses

Me: I know you are a sweet guy.[71]

Him: I have an X kids and stuff I really like u but

---

[68] I foolishly waited for him to call all day. I was an idiot.

[69] Money again. I can't stress how naïve I was.

[70] I wonder if he meant that. This was so confusing at the time because I trusted him. I was a fool. But you know, I trust everyone until they give me a reason not to. Keep reading.

[71] I am not sure about that. I had read some stuff that sometimes people are just confused about what they want.

That's why u pay for time baby[72]
emotionally I'm Not present for u[73]

Him: I'll be your friend but I need to heal Me Right this min

Me: Friends is great. I just want to get to know you better[74]
Take your time
I value the time we spent together
Please I know you're not blowing me off[75]

Him: Xo

Me: Patience is one of my qualities
So, when you are ready call me
Goodnight and Sweet Dreams.

Him: Kisses
Tomorrow
"insert smiley face from me"

Him: Fly me out or come out babe I need money
for my kids bottom line that's all I'm[76]
Thinking about right now

---

[72] Baby. I should have said fuck it when he called me baby. Baby is one of the most degrading nicknames. I am not your baby. I should have paid attention but I was in deep, emotionally.

[73] Another BIG red flag. I just laugh now because what else can I do?

[74] Did I seriously think things were going to work out? Yep, I did. Man, I am still laughing.

[75] Oh my gosh, really? Really? LOL.

[76] Money again. I am not sure what number that is. Way too many times, I can tell you that.

Have to go

Me: OK

Friday

Me: Good morning Andre. I know it's early but before work for me so I'm wide awake.

I have an ideal that may work out for both of us. When I arranged to see you, I did not expect to meet someone like you.

But it seems that I picked a bad time in your life to meet you. Which is unfortunate.[77]

I would like to see you again. If that would be ok with you let me know. And you can respond whenever. I know it's early. I just wanted to send this message right away.

I hope your day is wonderful.

Me: It's silly. I am thinking of you constantly.

Many hours later

Him: We can see each other through the Agency ok Hun

Me: Nope, I can't afford that. I guess I will move on.

Thanks for the wonderful time.

I knew I was a fool to hope for more.

---

[77] A little bit of sanity coming through but not enough, for sure.

At least I have great memories.[78]

Him: Your sweet your kind and a wonderful person[79]
and I'll be your friend
Xox

Me: I would love to be your friend really[80]
So, call me. But not now. I'm working. Laugh out loud.

Him: K lol

Me: Sounds good.
I finally took that video that you took of me out of the camera.
Me and the giraffe
You did a good job filming.

Him: Haaaaa
Thx lol

Me: I could forward it to you later via email when I get home if you want.
And I won't be offended if you say no

---

[78] I really would have been ok if he said goodbye then. I wish he had. I don't know why he wanted to hang on.

[79] I now realize that this is all true but it took a lot of pain for me to grow and realize this.

[80] I guess I would have taken anything at that time.

BTW, I am glad to know where we stand. I feel better.[81]

Him: Yes and ok
Glad
Send vid

Me: I will do so tonight.
Smiley emote big smile

Later that evening

Me: Sent

Him: Got it love it[82]

Me: Great. I wasn't sure about the email.

Him: At work now
Bartender part time

Me: I will leave you to it then. Talk to you soon. And have a great evening.

Him: Good night sweets

And two days later

Me: Smiling about the lack of room service at the Hyatt.
Big smiley emote

---

[81] I didn't know at the time how things would go so at the time, I felt better.

[82] It was a good video. And now it's a good memory.

Him: Lol[83]

> Me: It was funny.
> And they were way too late.
> I am not meaning to pry at all but are things going better?

Him: Lol

> Me: You cannot comment that last question if you want. (I used voice recognition and it mess it up).

> Me: I used that instead. My fingers aren't as good as yours. LOL.

> Me: If you don't mind, I suggest that we go on with our regularly scheduled lives. I really like you and you helped me to feel like a woman again. I visit Santa Barbara in April. Can I look forward to maybe seeing you then?
> I hope you don't feel that I am rejecting you. You need time for yourself right now.[84]
> Last text I promise. Texting just sucks. I did call and leave you a voicemail. I'd rather talk to you in person anyway. Texting sucks. It doesn't show good intentions.

I didn't hear from him again for 5 days. This is where I start

---

[83] One-word responses. I should have noticed and I think I was getting the clue but my emotions were crazy. But, you haven't seen anything yet.

[84] Again, I was trying to do the right thing.

stressing out about what is happening. I just didn't understand. I am a trusting person and couldn't see how he could be so nice and so not attentive. I was so confused. So, here we go. Emotions on overload!!!![85]

Friday

Today was a better day. I really doubt I will hear from him again. It was pointed out to me that I got what I paid for and, that for him, it's a job. Oh, yeah.

Reality sucks but I will move on. I really don't have a choice.

And you know what I am sad about? I finally find a guy who I felt like I connected with and was totally myself with and he accepted me as I was[86]. (Messed up emotionally, just broke up with his girlfriend, has no money, has a DUI – geez, when I spell it out like that, it doesn't look good). Who knows, maybe he was the world's greatest actor (as far as emotions goes) but man, he sounded sincere. I think I am a pretty good judge of character. His text confirms what he said to me. By the way, it's day 5 of no contact.[87]

I have turned this into a journal and I guess that is good. George[88] pointed out that I paid him for a job and he did his job. That is what he does. George does have a point. Should I ever contact him again?

---

[85] This is where the real-time journaling starts. As I felt them happening. It was a bummer at times.

[86] At this editing, I had found someone who accepted me as I am. It's not hopeless as I thought, at that time.

[87] I read online that you shouldn't contact a guy if he stops texting you to make him come to you. I have also learned that isn't necessarily true.

[88] George is a co-worker and my confidante in all things romantic. If I needed an opinion I would go to him because he was a guy and is better equipped to give me advice on men than my female friends.

At this point, I say no. But I do want to feel like I did with him again but it would be so hard not to get involved. It's like cocaine. I am an addict recovering and I should stay away from the stuff or I will get addicted again.[89]

What if he calls? Hahahahahahahahahaha. I don't think I will ever hear from him again.[90] I just hope that I am not just another notch in his belt and that he remembers me. I thought it was a special moment in time and I hope he does, too.[91]

Saturday

Ok, day 6 of no contact. I call Phoebe[92] to ask her about Christmas. And then she gave me all kinds of pointers of things that I already know. Man, that was a downer phone call, in a way.

I went to the store and I put on makeup and fixed my hair and made sure I was at least a 7 (or try to be)[93]. I was very confident in how I looked. I strutted around and remembered that I was "boned" just 2 weeks ago and I enjoyed it (and Andre didn't seem to mind at all – but that's a guy for you – and a guy who gets paid to do that).

See, to me, the money isn't an issue. Even paying him for his time because I got to meet him. Now, I would not pay to see him again.

---

[89] That is so true. It was like a drug.

[90] There are small doses of reality throughout and at times, I was sane.

[91] I am sure he doesn't remember me now but that's ok. I don't need him (to) anymore.

[92] My younger sister who is very bitter about men. She was right but I am glad I am not negative about men like she is. I decided to learn from this. Not generalize and make it about all men.

[93] I now know that I am a desirable woman. I don't care about a "number" system.

After all, I do have some dignity. But, if he did want to see me again in April, I would have to wait and see how I feel about it then.[94]

I wonder if it was all an act. If it was, man, is he good. I did get what I paid for, heartbreak and all. It was worth every penny though.[95]

It did teach me a lot about myself. How I was just sitting around, being mopey with no hope. Now I know there is hope for me to find that one true guy. Will it feel like it did with Andre? Oh, I doubt it.

There was something about him. I can't pinpoint it because if you look at his life, he is not doing that well (I think of the word Loser[96] but he is not a loser). He is just struggling with whatever and is highly stressed. And I think he might be an alcoholic? After all, he has a DUI. Speculation, it's a wonderful thing.

What if, in April, he got his act together? Not likely. People like that are on a self-destructive road. Until something wakes them up. But that sounds like a movie. A lot of times, I think things could work out like in the movies but then I remember, they are the movies. But they must have happened, one in a million?

But him, he made me happy. It can't just be him in the world though. Man, what a tough time this is. I just can't wait to talk to Anthony.[97] I hope I can keep it together when I talk to him. I will see what insight he has. What an unusual position I am in. Haha.

---

[94] When I was on vacation, he was in the back of my mind at times. It was just ego that wanted him to contact me. Not that I wanted to see him.

[95] I was talking about the chemistry we felt. Now, it's worth every penny because I learned so much about myself and I will never be that naïve again.

[96] More accurate than what I wanted to admit at the time.

[97] A friend that I met online that I play MMO's with. I have spoken with him for over 12 years even though we have never met in person. He's a good friend.

Sunday Day 7

Yes, I am counting it up. It's my thinking time. So, what do I think today? I talked to Anthony last night and he couldn't give me any advice at all. Or wouldn't. Either way, he listened to me rant on. I am sure by this April I will be over all this. I just don't want to be a fling.[98] But that is what I paid for.

I don't know. This is tough for me. On one hand, I know what I felt for him was real but I wonder if he was acting. I don't think he was and that is what no one else understands. It was a moment in time for both of us. A nice, sweet moment. His texts confirmed feeling for me, or at least a fondness for me – lol.

Him and he not being emotionally available.[99] He wanted to be friends. If it was an act, he is the biggest dick in the world, to mess with people's emotions like that. But I don't think he is a dick.[100] So, it must all be true (at least, at the time spoken). April will be the tell- tale sign. He isn't going to stop his life for me.

In fairy tales, let's see. He would get a fulltime job, stop drinking, get his license back just so he could be worthy of me – hahahahahahahahahahaha.[101] Oh crap, like that would happened. And he did it for me. I love movies. They are so romantic. Here's reality (probably). Around the end of March, he will contact me. He will see if I want to meet him again. I will ask him if I have to pay for time. He says yes and I say no thank you. I go on my trip to Santa Barbara solo. I really like the romantic example. But I am a girl. I was

---

[98] Fool, you paid for time and you got time!!! Of course, I was just a client.

[99] He told me straight but I was in denial. Like a lot of women do when they are presented the truth.

[100] He might have been. I really don't know him.

[101] I do deserve a good man.

conditioned through generations to feel this way. By the way, I am an idiot. I know nothing about this guy. I realized that right before I wrote the last text, that I had nothing to say to him.[102]

The more I think about it, the more foolish I feel. Ahh, but I thought we shared something. I will never know if it was real on his part. It was on my part and that is why I am having such difficulties with it. Onward and upward, I say.

Monday

Day 8. You know what? I know what I felt and I know he said he felt it and that should be good enough. Now, is this a good time? I would say no. But, maybe, maybe in April something good can happen.[103] And if not, what am I to do? Nothing. I am still going to Santa Barbara. So, help me, he better not be asking for money. It's his profession (well part time. He did tell me that it was 10 months ago since the last client and he really needed money this time around). I wish life was like the movies. Then I could have a happy ending (and so can he).

Ahh, he is so much younger than me. He will dump me for a younger version, a few years down the line. If it happens[104], that won't stop me but I probably will mention to him that I can see that happening. Oh, oh. We are in movie territory. Stop me!!!! Haha. Anyway, I did start the treadmill today like I said I would and I got my mammogram done. Tomorrow, womanly check-up. I should stay

---

[102] Why did I feel the need to text him again?

[103] Hope springs eternal.

[104] A so-called relationship.

on top of that and, from now on, I will. I must stay healthy as long as I can[105].

Day 9[106]

Oh, it's only day 9, I thought it was 10. So, how am I feeling today? I really must look at the reality of the picture. Yes, I am at that stage. I sure wish what we had could be long lasting. But it's probably better as a good memory. That's too bad too, because I really like him. But why? I don't know now (which is good, I guess).

Actually, he made me feel good about myself. I doubt very highly that he is thinking of me. So, I should stop thinking about him. The reason I don't want to is because I give up that feeling of joy I had when I was with him.[107] Like I said, it was like cocaine. I can remember it but knowing that I won't get that again is heartbreaking (yes, there are other men out there but he had something – something I haven't felt......[108]). Laura[109] called today and I did tell her the truth but I withheld some. It's better that I do. And that is why this relationship (non-existent) is doomed. Ahh, but it was fun. He really is below me. Can I just have a fling with him? Without my emotions? That is highly doubtful. I really must move on.

Day 10

I thought I would just start typing and see what happens. I don't

---

[105] I started to take care of myself for him but now I am doing it for me. The right reason.

[106] For some reason, I started counting days instead of days of the week.

[107] It wasn't real.

[108] Star Wars reference for all you geeks out there.

[109] Another friend. I have a few and they helped a lot during this crisis.

feel like I have healed that much but I feel that I am a whole lot better than last week. I was going to text Jasmine but I am not ready to talk to her. I don't really have anyone to talk to about this except George. He gives me encouragement to look to the future, whatever that may be.

I really must figure out what I want to do or what I should do or how I feel.[110] I still think Andre was sincere. It's just he has a whole different life and so do I.

Here is what I think. Judging and yes, I am judging but I don't know what else to call it. Oh, I know, I deduce that he really is that cool guy I was with but in his real life, he has a whole different persona. I saw the picture of his ex and I am nothing like her.[111] Not saying I am better. I really know nothing. Or is that what I wish? I think it's more so because I forgot about his DUI and he seemed like that he liked to party. Ahh, what do I know? See, all this speculation. Well, that is only because I don't know what is going on.

But, I am the one who said goodbye. I left it open for April. That is so far away. I am sure he won't remember me. I guess I am not special as I thought. At least to him. Ahh, self-pity. I can see all these things going on. I try to stay level headed and I am doing much better at work. But at home, I have nothing to do but think.

I did walk on the treadmill again. 30 minutes, 3.4 mph and I think the incline was at least 2. It was dark. And 1.61 miles. I will do it again on Friday. I have been putting some smiles on e-harmony.[112]

---

[110] I was confused. Even though I am in my fifties, I haven't had this experience before.

[111] Picture a blond, close to 40, nice smile and thin. She was what I would call the stereotypic Californian Blond, but not in a bad way.

[112] Let me tell you, e-harmony sucks. I ended up using Zoosk to find a new man.

I have very little hope in that but I must try. I still must figure out what I want to do. I need to change something.

At least I am starting with exercise and I will keep that up since I have figured a way to fit it in my schedule. And oh, yeah, let's not forget that I spent big money to feel this way.[113] Holy crap. This is tough. I will get through it. I am still not eating. This is not good. I will eat some fruit soon.[114]

Number Whatever Day

Oh, whatever day it is. I am not going to count anymore. I mean, what's the point? He obviously is doing one of two things. One, he is never going to call or he is waiting for April. I really hope I have found someone else by then.[115] I don't want to go begging back to him.[116] It just makes me sad.

You know, he did tell me he would call. Did he lie? But I told him that I would give him space and that was that. I sure left the invitation open for April though. It's hard to live in the now, since I was happy with him. But why? Why?

I realized something yesterday. That I was very comfortable being

---

[113] I literally banged my head against the wall in my shower, saying why was this happening? At least I didn't bang it hard. Gently, but with wall contact.

[114] I ended up losing 20 lbs. total from this ordeal. I just stopped eating. Now that I have lost the weight (which, by the way, was very easy since I was depressed), I am going to keep it off.

[115] I have. And he is great. The most wonderful man. He is nothing like Anaconda (He made a nickname for him. I was going to use if for the story but it sounded stupid. But I like the nickname so I wanted to make note of it).

[116] Nope, I have too much pride now to ever do that.

naked around him.[117] I wouldn't think that I would be so. What does that mean? Nothing. Haha. I am comfortable with my body.

I am still at an "I don't know" stage. You would think I would have moved on already. It's been almost 3 weeks since I saw him. Sigh. Man, I liked being with him. Not to be down on myself but he is a young stud, he can have any woman he wants. Wow, that is the truth right there. He did like me though. He told me so. And if he lied about that, he is the ultimate dick. Messing with people's feelings. I don't really know him so he could be like that. But my gut says no. I talked about this yesterday, too.

I am trying to find reasons to let go. I don't want to. It's not the misery I love, because believe me, this has been extremely hard on me. It's that I will be giving up feeling like that again[118]. I know, plenty of fish in the sea, blah, blah, blah.

I looked at some photos of him today. Probably shouldn't have. Ahh, what a pretty boy. Yeah, I could see why he would want to be with a blond type. I don't know anything again. Just typing my thoughts.

Hey, I didn't cry this morning and I only cried a little bit here.[119] I am getting better. Man, what an experience this is. I can't believe it. Normally, I am so level headed. This is so unlike me. Sigh again. I should have started journaling earlier. Oh well, I did the best I

---

[117] I went from a size 14 to a size 6 overall and I do look good nude now. So, I am confident.

[118] I don't get that high with my new man but I get something better, sincerity and honesty. And really great sex.

[119] I believe I cried every day for about 3 months and that is no exaggeration.

could but man, was I a mess that week anyway.[120] Probably best to forget that.

I decided that on e-harmony I would send out one smile a day. You never know. Whatever. I don't have much faith in online dating. Back to, I am an idiot. But really, I am not. Why do I feel this way??!!!!????? Ugh!!!!!! Audible sigh. Oh, I am doing better at work. More focused. I am stupid.

I sure feel stupid now. I paid him to make me feel good and that is what he did.[121] Ahh, I shouldn't forget our connection but it was long ago and far away now. Time to reflect – again.

No post yesterday (Friday)

Holy Shit!!!!!!!!!!! I am not kidding!!!!

Insert random internet blog that says horrible things about him[122]. True or not? I don't know but here is the reaction from that. The original writing had a website link but I am not going to do that to him. That would be too mean.

And this was posted on my birthday this year. Hahahahaha, it's so funny, I almost want to cry. It all was an act. Now, I am not going to feel guilty about it (at least at this point) because as I said earlier my emotions were all messed up. I mean, really bad.

Didn't I say he was a loser? I was right. I just had to see it for myself before I would believe it. Here are the two scenarios I see

---

[120] Immediately after I met him. The journaling started about 9 days after I met him and I had to remember the events as they happened. The emotional stuff here is real time. No memory for the emotions.

[121] I am sure he had no idea what I went through.

[122] I actually had more detail but I don't want it to be traceable so I deleted it.

going on. He contacts me, but what if he is that person (and what did I say about his persona earlier?).

Wow, I am perceptive and I knew it.[123] Emotions messing with my head. I saw it all. You know what, I have evidence that I was on a drug with him and was going through withdrawals and wasn't thinking straight.

Whenever I find a guy's real name out,[124] I google them right away and see what I find. That is how I have found a lot of BS out there (as far as online dating). But for some reason, I only thought of doing that today. And this sucks! But, hey, it's life, too. What did I expect? Ah, so I should treat the incident like Total Recall. A vacation memory that was fun but just an illusion. I like that. Now I did send him an email and a text. They both said the same thing.

Email below.

> *All I can say is wow. I really was a fool, wasn't I? Live and learn.*
>
> *You are a horrible person to do this to another person. You play with people's emotions for money or whatever else you do. How can you be like that? I fell for it too. This is what I get for being a nice trusting person.*
>
> *Once you realized that you weren't going to get any money from me he stopped replying or at least gave me one word answers. It's too bad too. I did like you but it must have been an act. Go on with your sad little life, I am sure that you are not happy but go ahead and pretend. It's what you are good at.*

---

[123] It isn't over yet.

[124] When I am dating online.

End of email.

His response was this

Hi,

I'm really not sure why your acting like this. First off, The agency is a service and biz and after we saw each other that is supposed to be it. I liked you as a person and agreed we could be friends and talk and maybe visit in the future. What more can you ask for? I treated you wonderfully and because I am busy with life and my kids doesn't mean I'm ignoring you. You have come on strong and money has nothing to do because I I said go through the agency if want to book and you wanted to meet off the radar. So tell me why in so bad and horrible? In terms of that posting it is bs and you don't know my background or situation. Look up my "The Most Popular Social Media[125]" and professional experience and you will see. I'm loving father and Christian. Anyway, it's the holiday season so if you want to act like the devil and not apologize for being mean to me than fine. I thought you were special and I was trying to really give you my heart and the way I could with such a short time meeting you. I was fine about seeing you in future. I'm sorry that your sad and angry.

I wish you love and peace and happiness with you friends and family.

Andre Xoxox

---

[125] You know what that is but I can't use it for legal reason.

And my response to that:

Holy Shit, I was wrong, so so wrong, I am so sorry. I am
so so sorry, Please forgive me. I am having a hard time
now and my emotions are all over the place.

Man, I wish I could erase what I wrote above and I am sure
not going to read it.[126] Probably ever. And his reply? Oh, boy, was I
wrong.[127] At least he forgave me. I know how he feels now. He felt the
instant connection too and he wants to stay connected with me.[128]
Man, so now I got what I wanted. Now what? It's funny, he knows
more about this stuff than I do.

I don't think I have ever felt this way about anyone before. It's
so odd. And why me? I mean, look at him. I am cautious but so far,
he has not been fake so I should enjoy it. Right? RIGHT? I mean,
com'on this guy is a catch.[129] You strip down all the bullshit around
him, he is a good guy. I just know it. He is what I have been looking
for. But to find it in such a wonderful shell is mind boggling. I mean,
really. Look at him. How did I get so lucky.[130] Man, I got to not ruin
this and over think this so I must go.

Christmas Eve

---

[126] Even in final stages of editing, I still can't read it. And I haven't and I might never
read it. I don't know what to say. It's just cut and paste but you guys enjoy it. Ha.

[127] Not sure if I was or wasn't now.

[128] I didn't imagine that connection. That was a relief to find out. If he was telling
the truth. I don't know.

[129] Umm, if he was normal, probably.

[130] You wish you were so lucky, at the time. Now I know it's a disaster walking. At
least for me it was.

The texting started again, and again I was naïve and I believed him. This is Christmas Eve.

Him: Please read your email

> Me: Why did I feel so bad. I just like you so much and I
> don't know what to do. [131]
> I'm sorry.[132]

Him: Babe
> It's ok and I did connect with you[133]
> And on my kid's life, my time with you was pure and
> honest[134]
> I want nothing but love and joy for you

> Me: I thought so

Him: I think what happened is for the good your realized maybe
> that love and happiness is possible again[135]
> I want to seriously be there for you and stay connected it's
> foolish to be any other way.
> Sorry I didn't respond right away but have been dealing
> with a lot with my kids and also positively been working

---

[131] I was crying up a storm. I should have let him go then but I was trusting. I am a good person.

[132] Why am I apologizing? The article was probably true.

[133] Still I wonder why he sent the things he texted to me. No wonder I was confused (not to mention gullible).

[134] I just realized what he said. On his kid's lives. That is a pretty profound statement. Maybe he did feel it but you know what? It doesn't matter.

[135] He finally said something that was true for me.

on my start-up which I got an investor feedback and its positive!

Me: Now as far as that goes you're going to laugh.
Now this is the truth my hobby is real estate.

Him: I would like to call you later today for real and say hi if that's ok?[136]

Me: Every day I go to the real estate sites and see what the prices are and what's selling for what

Him: Lol
Haa

Me: I have floor plan books in my house that I look at

Him: Oh wow
What a coincidence

Me: I never got a chance to tell you
I think it's a good idea but I have to look at it in more detail

Him: For sure

---

[136] Again, with I will call. Yep, sure.

Me: Great I think I could look at it from a financial point of view and see if there's anything that could be streamlined or something.[137]

Him: Will share when time

Me: Okay that's good. I am glad I did not imagine our connection. It was hard for me there for a while. Thank you for being patient with me.[138]
You are welcome to call me later. I would be very happy to talk with you. And once again I apologize.

Him: Of course Hun have good day and talk to you late. Xo smile :)))) I want to see it!!

Insert photo of me

Me: Sent

Him: There it is!!!
Beauty!
;)))

Christmas Day

Me: Merry Christmas Andre

Him: You too sweets!
With kids!!! You?

---

[137] I am always willing to help someone. That is probably why this happened. I give everyone the benefit of the doubt.

[138] I am too nice. Thanking him. What a fool was.

Me: I am going to be cooking dinner for my son and my mom and his dad is coming over to exchange gifts with Nathan.

How about I get a selfie of you?[139]

I would love to see your smile.

Two Days Later

Me: Hi

You know, I would happily and feely give you by heart but I don't think you are ready for it. And you did hint at that.

So, it's time to say goodbye. It makes me sad but I think it's for the best. You will always have a special place in my heart. Thank you for spending time with me. It was wonderful.[140]

Him: Hun I'm sick as a dog with the flu in bed last two days[141]
Feel horrible

Me: I am sorry to hear that
Like I said I feel so alone so I don't know what to do

Him: Going back to bed - understand how U feel ..

Me: Did you read my email by chance

---

[139] Still living in fantasy land.

[140] I wish he had said goodbye then. But then I wouldn't have grown.

[141] Now, he did look sick in his Christmas photos.

Him: I'm Sorry I can't be there for you now talk soon xox

Me: Okay please get better

Him: Haven't read email but will

Me: It was a very lonely email. Help prepare for it
Very glad to hear from you. I'm sorry you're sick. Talk
to you soon.

Him: Yes ok talk later

Here is the email I sent.

I will always tell you the truth. How I feel.

I actually feel all alone. I try to get advice from people and they are all negative. I try to remember how I feel about you but it's getting further in the past (see how crappy time can be sometimes?). And I know you are busy but too busy to say hi? And when you say you are going to call me, you don't. Why is that? Don't you know that I would love to talk to you? Honestly, I am not getting any positive (from you) reinforcement. I really want to believe and trust in you but you are not giving me anything to hang on to. You know, anything would be nice. Am I not worth it? Tell me and I will move on. If you pull away, it's better now than later. Don't get me wrong, I did feel that connection too but a memory is not helping me now (damn, that time again).

And each of our pasts, are just that, past. I would like to see what the future holds for us but I can't do it alone.

Just thought I would let you know.[142]

Later the same day

> Me: Home from work yay
> Are you feeling better this afternoon?

Him: Hi haven't been working ... At home in bed
Off to my class that I have to go feel like crap
So annoying flu

> Me: What kind of class?
> Yeah you really appreciate being healthy when you're
> sick

Him: It's for my dui program[143]

> Me: Okay
> We'll have a good time anyway as much as you can
> Basically, I'm just wishing you well
> Ttyl

Him: Will when I'm in a good space we can talk[144]

> Me: That would be fantastic[145]

---

[142] When I put effort into it, I can be very politically correct and emotional at the same time. I always try to be nice. Probably part of my downfall with this situation. That and naivety. Oh, and I can't read this either. I am a wuss but it just brings up bad memories and why should I do that to myself?

[143] At least he was honest about that.

[144] He never made it to that good space. Probably hasn't still but I don't know that.

[145] Forever the optimist.

Thank you very much

Dec 28TH

Me: OK, Thanks

Oops, that was for Nathan not you haha

A Week Later

It's what? A week later, I think. I had some weird experiences and I will write about those. I am trying to live in the now so I haven't been journaling but I do want to record some stuff. It goes on and on and on and on (Queue the Journey song now).

I heard from him on Christmas and then nothing after so I sent him an email that I was proud of writing. One day I will have to cut and paste it here. Let me check about it though.[146] Nope, so another future thing to do.

Fiona[147] is on my arm making it hard to type.

I had a strange experience last weekend. I had gotten my new Roger Hodgson CD and I was listening to "In the Eye of the Storm." And I was dancing. And for a brief nano-second, I was with Andre, dancing in the hotel room. It was the weirdest thing ever! I felt woozy and dizzy afterwards. I don't know. It really felt real. Like I was there. Time travel? Who knows? But the sensation was real. I never had that happen before.[148]

---

[146] It is now pasted above.

[147] Fiona is a long hair brown tabby cat. She is 15 years old and I have had her since she was 6 weeks old. She was supposed to be my son's cat but she bonded to me.

[148] Proof that I was crazy. Haha. But I swear, it happened as I described.

I told him goodbye earlier this week and he came right back.[149] I find this odd. Not Ood. LOL. Doctor Who. He told me that he would call me when he was in a better space.[150] I told him fantastic and that is the last I heard from him, about 4-5 days ago. When I think about things with my mind, I know he will call but why?[151] He can have anyone, why me? Man, I am pretty lucky.[152] Absence makes the heart grow fonder. I am waiting and I will not contact him. I have been doing good. So, what is it about him?

Oh, my overly emotional stuff went away in a breath.[153] That was another weird experience. I was stressing as I had been for 3 whole weeks and I was seated on the edge of my bed. I thought to myself (and Andre, if you ever read this -which I don't mind, it's what I felt at that moment and everything always changes),"Why am I obsessing about him again?" and I took a deep breath, exhaled and it was all gone. Just like that. I got to admit, this has been one hell of a ride.[154]

And I am smiling now because it has been. I mean, Tucson in general was great, but did I know that I would meet someone that I really like? And I know he is a good guy.

I do have a dilemma though. I don't think a real relationship can happen with our individual situations. So, I should decide, do I deny myself the pleasure of being with him just because there is no

---

[149] All I can say is this is stupid, really stupid. I can't believe the things I thought. Oh, well.

[150] See above texts.

[151] Honestly, Oh My Gosh, I am so embarrassed at this stuff. I cannot believe I was that gullible or something. It is so painful for me to edit but I got to do it.

[152] I'm sorry, my first reaction after reading that was "Shit!!!!!" and I covered my mouth. Oh, this is crazy funny. LOL. But it was me.

[153] I might have not been overly emotional, but I was still delusional. Hey, a rhyme!

[154] Oh Baby, you haven't seen anything yet.

commitment? I might never get a chance like this again (especially as old as I am – not that I feel old, the number is high), to be able to be in the company of an amazing man.

This is bad for me, too. After him, no one, and I mean no one on any of the websites match up to his level.[155] I look at them all and it's nope, nope, nope. I am in a bad place to be looking for men, (hamburger is not going to do it after Filet Mignon – lol), really but at least I am level headed now.[156]

I just should just wait and see. I love having a whole bunch of scenarios going on in my head. Well, I don't even know anything so that is all I can do, speculate. Well, that's all for now. It's New Year's Eve. I really hope that he texts me Happy New Year. I will see if he even remembers me. I don't know. Oh, I remember what I wanted to say. If this isn't the most unique situation!?! It all started with I am going to rent myself a guy. I wonder how it would have gone if I had chosen someone else. Not like this, that is for sure. I am glad that I chose Andre. The "best" choice for me. Man, if I can have him for a while, I will be the happiest woman in the world. [157]

New Year's Day

> Me: Happy New Year!!!! I hope this year is wonderful
> to you.

---

[155] Just in looks. My new man is wonderful.

[156] Everything from the last footnote up, please don't even remember it. I can't believe it. Why? Why? You got to understand I am laughing at this stuff because it is so laughable. But man, it happened. Therefore, it's a comedy to me. Or at least a lesson.

[157] I don't think it would have been good. At least I see that now. Whew, dodge a bullet there.

Him: You tooooooo!
May love and light bring you all[158]

    Me: Thank you so much
       You are so sweet

9:57 am

And that was the last I heard from him via text. We exchanged a couple of emails after that (including my masterpiece goodbye email).[159]

Sometime later but not sure when

I sent this email.

Andre,

    First of all, I really want to apologize for my behavior that last few weeks. I was really mean and not trusting myself. I am very sorry.

    I am not crazy with emotions anymore, too (that was a really weird, wild ride - never happened before). Earlier this week, I was sitting on the edge of my bed and I asked myself, "why am I doing this to myself?" I took a deep breath, exhaled and it was all gone, and the useless anxiety and stress just left. So, I am back to being me!!! Yay!!!!

---

[158] That was a nice thing to say.
[159] It was well written. You will get to it soon.

With that being said, I don't want you to feel pressure to call me. You will call me, when you call me (not meant at all in a mean way) and whenever that is (or isn't) is okay. And whatever communication level is fine with me. I don't really know what you are going through (and thank you for setting me straight on that). I know you are seeking that "good space" and I want you to find it.

I would like to request one thing though. Can I still see you in April when I visit Santa Barbara? You are an amazing person. I would like to feel that connection again (you know, just typing that, it sounds so cold but it is meant with all the warmth in my heart).

So, what do you think? Can I see you again?

Thank you for your patience with me.

Marie[160]

It's Tuesday (the start of a new year)

I have to see where I left off. One sec. Ahh, so, we didn't get into the last email I sent.[161] Haha. That one was releasing him of the pressure of having to call me. He replied, "That's very special and sweet". I try to be nice. He said seeing me in Santa Barbara would be a possibility. Who knows what I will feel like by April?

And remind me to never look at the internet again. And you know what I am talking about. It makes me sad. I don't know, what

---

[160] I must have been crazy to send this to him. Man, I was crazy. What was wrong with me? I am not like this. And another email I haven't read for the same reasons I didn't read the others. Too much emotion, since it was me.

[161] See above.

I should do about him? My heart says go, go, go. My mind, not so much. I know I am a great person but why does he think so? There isn't much he can get from me materially so I guess he just likes me.

I am in a holding pattern right now. He said he will call. I have no idea what we are going to talk about. I could talk about my feelings but no one wants to talk about that. Hpmhhh, men. LOL. I wonder how long it will be before he calls?[162] I will keep you posted. I know he is a good guy (and I really like him – since who knows who else will read this so, honestly), I actually love him and it's one of the most stupid things I have done in my life.[163] But I can't help it. I am utterly drawn to him. It's like he feels like home, so safe, or warm or comforting, all those things. I want to make sure that he is happy and happy with himself. I can assume so much but I know nothing so I will not write those thoughts down.

Anyway, I am going to bed now. Don't know when I will be back. This is the most interesting time in my life, no doubt about it. And I am smiling. I might as well. After all, it might never happen again so I shouldn't worry. I can do it. Oh, and one more thing…Jackie. That video of him when he was younger is so cute. He wants to meet all the hot chicks. Which is exactly what a good looking young man would think. Smile again. On that note, goodnight.[164]

Tuesday

---

[162] Forever.

[163] Insanity, but at least my logical side knew I was crazy. See? I am not like this but I was. I won't be like that again.

[164] Boy, I am glad I am done editing that part. I sure was delusional but optimistic at the same time.

And it's over. I emailed him because I had made reservations. I will cut and paste the emails here for memories sakes.

Me to Andre:

> *Hi Andre,*
>
> > *My vacation plans are below.*
> >
> > *I am in no-way assuming anything. I always go to Santa Barbara for my vacation (as you know) and I usually plan everything way ahead of time so I thought I would let you know.*
> >
> > *I really hope things are going well for you. I care about you. I want you to be happy in your life.*
> >
> > *Call me when you will.*
> >
> > > *Still thinking of you,*
> > > *Marie*

Andre to me:

> *Hi Marie,*
>
> > *How are you sweetheart!*
> >
> > *Listen, if you want to meet fine.*
> >
> > *However, you need to book in through the agency.*
> >
> > *I provide a service and that is how I supplement my situation.*
> >
> > *I appreciate you and want to spend time, however I don't have the time to just get together outside of work hours.*
> >
> > > *Xoxoox*[165]

---

[165] Sorry, that was the most formal piece of shit email I have ever gotten. Really? I thought he was nicer than that or whatever. It was rude.

Me to Andre:

Ahh, Ok, I guess not then. I know that is how you make money. And it was great being with you. I want more than you can give and that's ok. I am reasonable now. I hope your life is wonderful because you are a good guy.

Andre to Me:

Yes, I'm sorry. I think you're a wonderful beautiful soul and I would love to give myself in the ways you need. However, that's a relationship or further interest that deserves commitment and attention which you sooooooo deserve. I just can't provide that right now. Xo[166]

Me to Andre:

Thank you so much Andre
    I'll just tell you right now. Unfortunately, I fell in love with you. It's my own fault. I thought meeting you would just be happy roll in the hay (and it was fun) but it didn't turn out that way for me. I know our situations aren't conducive for anything really.
    I will be ok because I knew deep down it was just a fantasy. What a fantasy it was.[167]
        I wish you love and happiness.

---

[166] At least this was more genuine.

[167] Trying to be a realist at the moment. It was the truth but I had a hard time accepting it – really soon, too, in the story. I think I cracked there for a bit. Man, it was intense.

Marie

And maybe I shouldn't have sent that last one, but what the hell, it was the last one. He might as well know. Yeah, I am sad. I know it probably it wouldn't have been good for me but I am crying anyway. Ahhhhh, love lost.[168] Well, my love goes unanswered. But I am glad that I sent that email because I know now. I really know. So, I would have been waiting for him to call and he never would have.

This is for the best. I know it. But it doesn't stop me from feeling sad. So much potential?[169] I am still going to Santa Barbara. It will be a bittersweet trip but that is only if I left now. In a few months, I will be fine.[170] He knows when I will be there. There is a small hope that he might want to see me but that is because the wound is still fresh (3 hours). After, he will fade.[171] And I guess that is what I am sad about. But I do have it all documented. I won't forget.

Oh, how sad I am right now. Over what though? Com'on girl, get it together. I will. That is why I am doing my last journal entry, because it is over.[172] I do not want to ever go through this again. Ok, what a comparison I have now. I mean, really. Oh, well. I did this to myself. But I didn't know. I just didn't know. What a fool I am. But not twice, I tell you. I will be very careful. So, now what? I just go on. I feel sad about my situation but Eli[173] died Sunday and that is 10 times worse than what I am going through. So, God, I am very

---

[168] Never had, I guess? It was all in my mind. So unlike me.

[169] Potential for what? Never give up! Never Surrender!

[170] I was totally fine. I had a great trip.

[171] Poof!!!!

[172] But Wait!!! There's more!!!!

[173] He is my 9-year old grand-nephew. He had Neuroblastoma.

grateful for my life. I guess this was just a lesson I needed to learn. So, what did I learn?

The biggest thing I learned: Don't have sex with someone.[174]

The above was the only negative I could think of (and that includes all the crap that comes afterwards).[175]

I learned that I can still be sexy. [176]

I learned that I am good looking and I will be at least a 7 when I go out.[177]

I learned that I fall in love too easily. I was a sucker. I knew it.[178]

It's not that he doesn't want to, because his texts say otherwise. It's that he is so messed up that he can't. Boy, I sure do pick them.

I was going to type a whole bunch of questions, but why? I will never know answers so I do not need to burden my soul with them.

This is going to be my last entry and I am sad. Man, it was so fun, and joyful, heartfelt and close and horrible and aggravating, and so much of everything – more good and bad. What a trip it was. And I am sad that I won't get my fantasy. Oh, well. There must be something waiting for me. But Andre, he will always be my fantasy guy. The guy I had such a great time with. I won't forget. Thank you, God, for that experience. I truly appreciate it.

And there is nothing else to say. I guess this is it. I am going to cry long and hard on the bed and move on.

---

[174] Oh, when I said I had great sex with my new guy earlier, that was a lie! *wink* *wink*

[175] I never went through it again. It was a weird experience. So, it was just him? But Why? I will never know but I didn't like being that out of control so I don't want it to happen again.

[176] Hell, Yeah!

[177] As we all say, "For my age, I am looking pretty good!" But I am.

[178] This was not easy. Not by a long shot.

Thank you Andre, ~~for your love~~. [179]

Last email, because I had to.

Ahh, Andre,

You will always be that great guy I had the most wonderful time with in Tucson. It was so nice being with you. What else can I say?[180]

I really do hope that your life is full of love, happiness and joy. You are a caring, sweet guy and you have much love to give. I know it.

So, this is my closure email. I have to write it and send it. And no reply is needed. I just don't like leaving things unsaid.

But I don't think there is much else to say. I will remember you always (yes, I know in time the memory fades, but when I think of Tucson and/or hear a Supertramp song, I will smile[181]).

Thank you for our time together. It really was a remarkable experience that changed me for the better.[182] I am really glad we met. J Farewell.

Love, Marie[183]

---

[179] I really wanted to delete that line but it's part of the story. But it's so embarrassing, too. I just shake my head at times.

[180] He was this. I did have a great time with him.

[181] I don't think of him anymore and I still listen to Supertramp.

[182] So true.

[183] I am proud of this email. It doesn't point fingers and it just says how I felt about meeting him. If it was just that, the positive parts, it would have been the best experience in my life. But it came with all the bullshit afterwards. Bummer.

Wednesday

So, it's the next morning. I called in sick to work. I really can't go in. I had like zero sleep and my head was aching from crying too much.

By the way, he sent me an email saying, "cry your amazing". I emailed him back saying, remember, I am just me. And I called which I regret but he didn't answer.[184] He has never answered. I have not heard from him and I don't suspect I will. And I sure won't contact him because it's time to let go. I said I would today so I must. All the future plans were just fantasies. But I do have that wonderful memory and I am glad that I recorded it all here. One day, I will look back on it fondly. I can smile. I really do like my closure email. It said exactly what I wanted it to. And that is that.

The email I never sent is below.

> *Goodbye Andre,*
>
> *It really was great meeting you and spending those moments together. You taught me a lot, too. More than I knew about myself. I hope you have a great life. You will be a true love but it is not meant to be.[185] At least I felt it for a brief moment. Good luck with your life. I hope you can get it together and realize that you are better than selling yourself for money. You really are. There are lots of things I never got to say to you and I never will. I'm apologize I fell in love with you. I didn't expect to and*

---

[184] It's still early in the obsession.

[185] I thought so at the time. I don't know if I have found my true love yet (talking about the guy I am seeing now). It would be nice if he ended up being so. I like him a lot.

it sure did complicate things for me. So, as reluctant as I am, I am going to end this and say goodbye, because it is goodbye. I wish that moment could have lasted forever. Damn Time.

Love forever (in some form),

Marie

Man, that made me cry. LOL. So, it's now Saturday, and I am captured by a delicate thought. A fancy........ I love that reference.[186] Anyway, I came here to write down my thoughts since I sent that email. I can recite that email[187] from memory now. It is a masterpiece. LOL. It was positive all the way.

I realized that he really did change me for the better. Since I met him, I lost weight (and yes, 9 lbs.[188] in 5.5 weeks is not healthy but boy, was it easy). I am taking vitamins. I am going to buy me some roller blades. I got all my health exams. I dress better. I wear makeup when I go out. I am at least a 7 in the public (except for work – but I still try to dress nicer). He was good for me in that way.

I wonder why he had to come along with all that baggage (yes, he had some already but I am talking about the stuff I came away with after meeting him). I know why. It's that connection. It's why I don't really want to give up on him.[189]

Ahhh, he would have to change to be with me and I don't think he can. I know in movies he would change his life and come back

---

[186] Alan Parsons Project – Tales of Mystery and Imagination by Edgar Allen Poe – Beginning of side 2 – yes, an album.

[187] The one I sent (the masterpiece), not one I did not send, (right above).

[188] After all of it, I lost 27 lbs. and I am happy. Not the best way to lose weight but it worked. And I will keep it off, too.

[189] I am so happy I have moved on.

better. I know that if he wanted to come back[190] I would have to take it so slow. I can't do this again. I really can't. It's 6 weeks (tomorrow but I don't journal every day now) and I still think of him constantly. It is getting less though.

He did the most wonderful thing in letting me go.[191] I know he cares and that is why he did it. I knew (yes, past tense) he was a good guy. I wish I didn't have to let him go but I do. Man, here I go again crying. Good thing I can type with my eyes closed. Hey, I did pretty good. :-D Only one error, A missing letter.

Any more thoughts? Oh, I am working on living in the now. I have to. I can't wander off to fantasy land. I am still going to Santa Barbara.[192] I don't know why. Hoping? A small amount. But mostly I hope I don't hear from him again because I might as well type it. He is my Kryptonite. My big, big weakness. Ahh, I feel the forces pulling us together. Is that silly?[193] We will see. I can't contact him. He must contact me and I don't think he will ever be ready? Time heals the thoughts. I wish time would go by already. But 4 days isn't enough. Look how long it took to get back to sane. And you're sane now. Wow, this is bad. Ok, on to the now. Going to brush my teeth and walk Bubbles. Until next time.

Sunday

Time for more reflection. I figured something out in the last few minutes. I understand why our time was special. Since we didn't

---

[190] Hahahahaha *gasp for air* Hahahahaha. What a fool I was.

[191] Why was I so naïve? That is what I want to know.

[192] I never changed that plan. Santa Barbara is my vacation spot and I am not changing it for anyone.

[193] Ummm, Yeah. LOL.

go in with any expectations of who the other person was, we, each individually, got to be the people we really are, without all the stuff in our lives that brings us down. So, we were our true selves. And that is why we connected. I think I touched on this earlier in this writing.

There is so much. I am on page 37. Hahahahahahaha. If you would have told me in the beginning of December, that I would be writing a lot of stuff, I would have laughed. Would I warn myself about Andre if I could? I don't think I would. The experience was life changing for me. And I think for him, too.[194] I knew he was a good guy. I am sure that I have typed that before. But you know, he did say now[195]. But that is just me doing the wishful thinking thing.

But for some reason, I think I am not done with him.[196] But he should contact me. I cannot contact him. If he ever does, I am going to ask him pretty much right away if he found that "good space" yet? I hope he does. Man, I still think of him way too much. It's hard to stay in the now. It's a constant battle. It really is. Do I want to be tempted again? I hope not. I hope he fades soon. Why? Because this is really painful for me. And this is really stupid, too. Man, I only spend 6 hours with him. Why? Why? Why? See earlier in paragraph. Haha. The longer I go without hearing from him, the sooner I will give up on thinking I will ever hear from him. [197]

Tuesday

---

[194] Oh, I am pretty sure nothing has changed for him. I have no ill will towards him.

[195] Referring back to his email where he said that he didn't have time for me now. He really meant forever.

[196] Why I thought I was anything more than a client, I have no idea.

[197] Now that is a correct statement. If I wasn't writing this, I don't think I would think of him at all.

A week after the closing. This is probably the best. I looked on the internet and found some photos of him modeling. It was in interview with some chick (horror, goth stuff) and she mentioned that they had great chemistry. I am not sure when the photos were taken but the article was written after I met him. So, what does that tell me? I am probably a fool and this is good for me to see this. I don't think I should see him again. I will not try and justify what I saw. I saw what I saw. What if he has great chemistry with everyone? I don't want to be in a line of women he has conquered.[198]

Now, I have reason to doubt which is the best thing that can happen to me. I don't know. Again. Man, I said goodbye. It's got to be goodbye. My prospects on Match.com suck. Oh, well, I am not going to put any effort into it. The man must chase me. I am not chasing a man and that includes Andre. My kryptonite. If he is a good guy, he will not contact me again. I want to get over this.

I am stupid (I don't really think that but man, sometimes, I do have to wonder). I don't want any hope. That's better. He has his life and he told me straight out that he doesn't have time for me. And what was up with that email? Repeat, I know. But really? Move on, Woman. You are better than this. You are. Man, am I messed up mentally. I am having a hard time shaking these feelings for him. It's only a week. I hope it doesn't take too long. But my closing email is how I should see things. It's final and I must remember that. And I wrote it. Memories only, no future. It was a lot of fun. Sigh.

Wednesday

So, I have decided that I don't want to be part of his lifestyle.

---

[198] I don't think now that he conquered me. Just things turned out unfortunately.

What I mean is, I don't like his lifestyle and he would have to change it drastically for me to accept it and I just don't see that happening. I am sad about that. But at least he got a peek at what it looks and feels like to have a real person (and love).

I am sure it changed him as much as it changed me.[199] What I am sad about is that he won't ever see what positive changes I have made in my life because of him.[200] Ahh, Andre, again.

So, I went and checked out Match.com. I am chatting with one guy and he asked where I have been on vacation and am I planning any? My first reaction was to reply with this, "Yeah, I am going to Santa Barbara to see if this guy I slept with once to see if he wants to sleep with me again." Hahahahahaha. Man, sometimes I make myself laugh. I did tell him I am going there though. I think I have moved on finally but I still have strong feelings for him. I wonder when that will fade.[201]

I sure do wish he wasn't where he is. He is not happy. I just know it[202]. And I know he's trapped but he has got to fix it. I can't do it. Ahh, com'on Andre, don't do it for me, do it for yourself so YOU can be happy. You look so sad in that photo.[203] There is no happiness at all. So, another dilemma.

What if he does contact me?[204] I mean, he has bounced back many times. I must remember that he must be in that good space

---

[199] I wouldn't count on that, baby.

[200] That's my ego speaking.

[201] I would say it was 4 months.

[202] I don't know shit.

[203] A photo I saw on "The Most Popular Social Media". Yes, I was stalking him but trying not to.

[204] I am still in fantasy land. I am so logical in real life. Man, oxytocin. It's some powerful stuff. I guess.

for him to do so. And I don't know about that. But if he does? Then, what do I do? I mean, if I don't expect anything, will it be that bad? Hmmm, yes. Remember? Just go back up about 10 pages. Ahh, yes. I hope he misses me at least.[205] I am amazing. He knows it. Him? I know deep down he's good but his life, man. Anyway, done beating the dead horse. Until next time (whenever that is).

Yay, Thursday

How do I feel today? I am not sure. I have come to the realization that it is over between me and him. But why do I still love him? Why did I love him in the first place? You know, I don't have answers for that.[206]

But just being with him for a short time changed me. And it was really sweet that he tried to keep contact with me. Ahhh, it was destined to fail. And there it is in a nutshell. Ahh, Andre. You won't get to reap the reward of what you did for me. Or will you ever know and that is what I think is sad. Will you get your life together? I know he is trying, I think. I know nothing except he doesn't have time for me. And that is the bottom line. I guess that's all for now.

Saturday

Man, this is so messed up. I am still thinking of him constantly. And hoping that I can see him in April. How bad is that? What

---

[205] Nope. Maybe a little at the time (a wee amount) but now, I don't think he even remembers my name. I have changed all I could to keep his identity a secret. No need to embarrass him either. I am sure he had no idea what I was going through. I didn't know what I was going through.

[206] Even after all this time, I still don't know why this happened to me. But good story, heh?

happened to me? I can think logically and write all that stuff down (just see all the many paragraphs above) and I still want to see him. UgHHHHHHHHHHHHHHHHHHH!!!! I am literally shaking my head "no" as I write this. I am all stressed out even though I try to hide it the best I can. I am upbeat around other people. It's when I am alone that my brain starts wandering. And wondering.[207]

I have been getting more exercise in my life. I will walk around instead of sitting if I am waiting for something. My weight has been consistent at 124.8. And I can smile about that. I have been maintaining that. Since it was so easy to lose (you know, when you're not eating), I am going to keep it off.

Why wasn't he a normal guy? I wouldn't have met him if he was. Ahh, so messed up is he. Hey, Andre, if you ever read this (hahahahaha), I never would want to hurt you but I can tell you what I think is happening by all the evidence I have. I might as well run it all down for you readers out there. *deleted BS gone*.[208] Remember, this is all speculation and I can be wrong. See, this is all BS. I don't really know anything but what I found. I am going to erase all that. Haha.

I know that someone on the internet accused him of using her and dumping her. They also accused him of being bi-sexual. I did notice that on the comments, no one knew him except the original poster. Andre said the story was BS.

I also saw photos recently of him posing with some chick (see above). Every time I think of that, I get jealous (yeah, I shouldn't, I

---

[207] I was obsessed but at least I am sane now.

[208] No one wants to hear all the excuses I can make up. I did delete the stuff at the time of the original writing. I knew it was BS.

know – he does what he does).[209] And see, he is better than that. I know he is, deep down. But his situation dictates what he does (and he should break free). I know the most recent photo of him on "The Most Popular Social Media" is sad. I do wish I can save him, but I can't. See, all these feeling are here but I have no one in the real world to express them to. Ahh, I am foolish. I think I am going to go walk to Kohls. The weather is blustery. I like that. I need more pants that fit.

No pants. Nothing fit. Anyway, I am not sure why I am back this evening. I am listening to Roger Hodgson, Lovers in the Wind. It's a beautiful song. I am distressed that I can't get over him.[210] It's just so stupid. Man, at this point, if he called me in April to meet him, I would say yes, and that would be so bad for me.[211] Why him? I do wonder if he is saying the same thing.[212] Ahh, who knows. I know nothing. I came here to type that I hope he never contacts me.

I am so weak with him. I hope someone else comes along. Someone else wonderful. It might never happen[213]. A thought that I had today that I had before is that if he did call (I don't know where I was going with this – carry on). I can't call him even though I think of ways that I can call with some stupid line but then I remember

---

[209] Ahh, I see him now and he isn't that attractive. I really was enamored.

[210] I did. It just took some time. Reading back on this stuff, it reminds me of how messed up I was but now, it is just like a dream. But I really felt and wrote these things.

[211] Logic creeping in. I was fighting it all the way. Emotions, man. Sometimes they lead you awry.

[212] No, again, you fool. He didn't think of you.

[213] But it did!!!! And I really like him!!!

that I don't want to look desperate and if he wants to see me, he will let me know.[214] I don't want to intrude.

I wonder though. Is the pull strong on his side? I know that I said goodbye 3 times and he always came back. So, I think it is. What do you say? I think I will hear from him. Or is that just wishful thinking? It's still 3 months away. I read somewhere that it is the idea of him that I love, not him.[215]

Well, if you think of him realistically, he is not a prize but I know he is a good guy (really).[216] So, it's him because when I think of what he does, it's really depressing. It is. How could a guy that I love (yes – ugh, I can't help it and it's not fading …yet),[217] think that he needs to sell himself for money. Oh, if he only didn't have to feel that he needed to do that. I don't. Maybe he's happy and all this crap I am writing is just writing. But no, I remember what he texted to me early on. I swear, this stuff is aging me (it might just because I don't have so much fat on my face so it's sagging, ugh).

"I may not love you, but I can't stop thinking of you. Give me love, give me life, give me hope, get me up, get me up and dancing again. Give me time, give me reason to hope!!!!!" Thanks, Roger.[218]

Monday

---

[214] And he doesn't. He probably thinks I was crazy.

[215] I don't know to this day what it was about him.

[216] I do believe that he had a good heart but was trapped. Mainly by his huge "anaconda". It started young and it just rolled along.

[217] I am so glad I am over him.

[218] I am back to editing, after a week's break. Oh, this is so painful for me. To think I was this naïve but I swear, it must have been hormones or something. This is not me. I never want to be this person again, I can tell you that. On with the tale of woe.

Man, if life isn't just the most interesting thing? So, I got an offer for free sex!!!!! Yes, Freee!!!! And from a cute, in shape guy. Hahahahahahahaha. And he's younger than Andre, I think he's 35. Oh, wow!!!! I have so many conflicting emotions but I must remember that Andre told me to move on. He did. I still kind of feel guilty that I am considering it. Should I consider it? I must weigh the pros and cons.

And can I have sex and just walk away?[219] That is what I want to know. See, that will tell me whether it was Andre or just any guy. I will set up rules right away so things don't get messy. I don't want messy. I want to forget Andre.

I can't believe that I am considering this but nothing else is working. Am I expecting too much from myself? I got to admit though, this is distracting me. I don't have to decide right away. I will think about it for a couple of days. I guess this is all thanks to Andre. But I don't want to start sleeping around. Really. I am a high value woman. So, if we do it, it will be on my terms. Yes, I will have terms. Like, I don't want to hear from him for at least 3 weeks. Or should I just play for a bit? Yay, Supertramp!!! Rick Davies. Anyway, that's all for now. There's nothing else to say.

Tuesday, the 24th

Two weeks since I said goodbye. And you know what? I am ok with it. Why? Because I have a distraction. Smile. I set up a "meeting" for the 11th of February. And wow, if my life hasn't turned into a soap opera. I mean, really. I have NO ONE to talk to. So, I do

---

[219] I sure can. No doubt about that. What was it about Andre that just drove me crazy?

this journal. I am eager about meeting this guy. No names. I want this to be just sex.

I need to forget Andre and this is the way. I know it will work because it is already working. And maybe, if closer to the date, I change my mind, I can. I think this will be an interesting experience. He did offer himself to me so I must be worth something. He has flirted with me before, too. I am worried if he is going to use me. Yes, he is going to use me. Hmmm, isn't that what I am doing? I am using him as a tool to forget Andre. I wonder how it's all going to go down. Too many questions, no answers. At least it's far away enough that I can treat myself and be able to "do it".

This is going to be great. Well, I think it will be. It will serve its purpose and I must remember the 3-week rule. Wow, just two days ago I was pining away for Andre. Now it doesn't matter. I did need something else. Anything else and he will do for now. Not Mr. Right but Mr. Right-Now will do. And it will be a learning experience. Yep. Wish me luck. [220]

Wednesday

I am just here to fill up space, not literally, just on paper (computer). Jasmine is back but I don't want to talk to her. I mean, what am I supposed to say? By the way, I figured out a way to forget about Andre. I am going to go have sex with this other guy. That will fix it.[221] Hahahaha. Yeah, it does sound bad.

---

[220] OH, DID I LEARN MORE THAN I WANTED TO. His nickname is now "Tiny dick". And he was a dick and it was tiny. That's all you need to know. LOL. It didn't happen when it was originally scheduled but it did happen. What a mistake. That is all I have to say about it.

[221] It didn't fix it but at least I know I can do it without getting emotionally involve.

This guy will be number six on the long list of guys I have slept with in my life. I know, not a huge number. Got married in high school, stayed with him for 21 years. Two brief affairs (one was longer but they both were a waste of time) and a boyfriend (if you could call him that, more like f*** buddy and he would fix things around my house – he was married, of course) for 14 years. And then Mr. Wonderful (and he really was Mr. Wonderful). And this new guy, who I am going to use to forget Mr. Wonderful.[222] Even though I am distracted by the fact that I am going to "do" this guy (which I admit, is exciting – I get to get dressed up and wear my nice stuff again. Yay!!!), my thoughts still wander to Andre. I hope to stay in the moment with the new guy.

Ahhhh, Andre. I was going to type, I wish it was you, but really, do I? If only he was normal. But that is not reality. Sometimes reality really sucks. I know, things can be a lot worse. I was telling people today that my life has turned into a soap opera. Really. And this is all because I wanted to go to Tucson and rent "company". Joseph[223] said that he did his job. And yes, he did. But he is more than that. I know that. He's a good guy that I won't hear from again. I really hope not. I don't think I could deal with it again.

But you know secretly, I wish he would contact me. Even if I have to turn him down. Could I turn him down? I hope I never find out. I haven't had any meeting fantasies in a while. The distraction is working. Good thing I don't write down all my thoughts because

---

[222] I know I say this a lot but man, I was out of my mind. I don't know what I was thinking. It's crazy. Ok, onward.

[223] Another co-worker.

yes, they went into fantasy land, just for a moment. This is still a struggle. [224]

I hope I learn whatever lesson I am supposed to learn from this mess. It is so weird to have this happen to me. To me? Yes, me. This is all happening to me. Hahahahahaha.[225] At least I am confident enough to have sex with a stranger (yes, I have met him a few times before). That is thanks to Andre. I really like my goodbye email to him. I didn't blame anyone for anything. It just isn't going to work out. Ahhh, my fantasy guy. He is going to stay that way. I guess that's it for today. It might be a couple of days before I write anymore. I don't think much is going to happen (yep, right).

Thursday

Not much going on. I did find the new guy on "The Most Popular Social Media." Not much else to say. I feel kind of bad for Andre.[226] I am getting further away. I know if I saw him again it would all come rushing back.

Friday

I am kind of melancholy right now. I am finally getting a grip that I won't see Andre again. At least I am talking about him in

---

[224] I was inventing lots of unlikely scenarios. You know how us women are. When we want, we will believe things that aren't true.

[225] Even though I went through all this, it is like a dream now. I remember it but it's not relevant to my life right now. I have learned my lessons.

[226] WHYYYY??? I really want to know.

past tense now (sorry, Andre).[227] But I am sure that he is doing fine without me.[228]

And I am doing pretty good, really. I am planning my liaison so that is distracting me. I must remember that I don't want a relationship. I am feeling a little empty. I don't want to project my feelings for Andre on him. I must remember my list when I get there and stick with my requirements. It will be the best. I hope it's a good time.[229]

I wonder if anyone can relate to the stuff I am writing. I posted on "The Most Popular Social Media" that I am writing a book and I got a positive response back. One of Nathan's friend's mom said that she can't wait to read it. Wow, I don't know if she really wants to read it. This is going to be for a special kind of audience.

It sure is an experience going through all this. Before my life was dull. I did the usual stuff every day that all people do. But I didn't really have anything that I wanted to live for.[230] Andre changed that for me. Thank you, Andre. If you only knew what you did for me. Of course, this will be dedicated to him.[231]

I wonder if he would even know that I wrote about him. What will people say when I publish this? I expect it to be published. I don't think anyone else has been through this exact situation and to think it all happened to me.

---

[227] Oh, he's fine without me. He didn't need me. But I needed this experience to grow, so here it is. Printed out for the whole world to see.

[228] Yep, whatever. Haha.

[229] It was the most disappointing sex I have had in a long time.

[230] Not that I was suicidal or anything. It's just that life was uneventful and so there was nothing to look forward to.

[231] I am not sure that I will dedicate this to him. He was important but he doesn't deserve the book dedicated to him.

I do find it comforting that I did find someone that I connected with on such a deep level. He was just there for those moments but it mattered so much. I can't ever call him. And I highly doubt that he will contact me. But I do suspect that he misses me.[232] This is such an odd place for me to be in. I am dealing with it the best I can. I still am disappointed that I must go to extremes to forget him. I told myself that I will finish this book in April. [233]

I wonder if my life will be roller coaster until then. If it is, 2017 will be an exciting time. I realize that editing this will be very painful for me. I hope by the time I reach that stage, all these feelings will have fallen into place and I can look at what I wrote objectively. Sometimes, I think I am crazy but I try to keep it together. I tell you, that I am so much better than a month ago. Wow, that last time we texted was almost a month ago.

Ahh, he is a good guy. I am glad that he let me go but know I am out here with these new feelings and ambitions and zest for life by myself. What am I supposed to do now? That is not a desperate plea. It's literally what am I supposed to do now? I am on Match and eHarmony. What a waste of time that is.

I am living the best I can. And I am trying to take care of myself. I am still skinny, I have been taking care of my health. I am confident in how I look now. I never go out in public less than a 7 (except maybe work – which is a 6). Joyce said I was attractive yesterday. I guess I am. I did attract a man a lot younger than me.[234] I don't know

---

[232] Nope, still in denial but I am getting better!!!!

[233] In other words, the story will be finished in April. It's taking a little longer than I thought to go through it all.

[234] For money. I mean, I look at the text and sometimes I wonder but it still was a fantasy, no matter how you look at it.

exactly how old but I will write it down as soon as I find out. Hey, more stories upcoming!!!! Oh, I got to go. Write more in the future.

A day later (not sure when it was, really)

This morning I am feeling happy and sad. I am so happy about the memories that I have with Andre.[235] I was recalling when I was telling him how happy I was that he was here just for me (and yes, I did use those words because he was!). He was all smiles. It was great.

Now I am sad because it's only a memory. But man, it's one of the best.[236] Carry on.

Later this evening

I just want to share this thought (it's a happy one). I know that in life when you choose a mate, they (and you) might be ideal in the beginning and then they just let themselves (and maybe yourselves) go (I am talking physically). So, the opportunity to be straddling a guy with a perfect body (I really didn't see one flaw) is so exciting. And it really did make me happy. If only I could explain the intense connection we had. Yeah, I hate using past tense but I have to. I don't see a future. But the past was awesome!!!

It was second best experience in my life. Of course, my son has the top spot.

I am so much better now. I feel good about myself. I have a dilemma. I have the nice black nightie that I wore for Andre and it does look good on me but I feel like I would be betraying him if I

---

[235] I honestly don't think of him during my daily life any more. If I wasn't writing this, I probably wouldn't think of him at all.

[236] I am making better memories. And these are real, not a fantasy.

wore it for someone else.[237] Truth be told, it's in a bag in my closet. I haven't washed it yet. Yeah, way too sentimental. I will probably tomorrow.

That is really the last thing that I have that is original, if you know what I mean. All other things from that trip have moved, changed, been washed, etc. Sigh. I am silly sometimes.

On to now.[238] I have my whole outfit figured out. I will probably change it last minute. I did get a nice shirt that is sheer (I have a camisole I can wear under it or I can wear just a bra. It's very feminine. I like feminine.

George suggested that I wear jewelry which is a great suggestion. So, I got some new matching pieces. I have lots of earrings but not any matching necklaces and earrings.

Back to the clothing. I have this black dress that is long and knitted and I have never worn it because it is a winter dress. I will wear that with either red bra and panties or maybe the rose color set I have. That's classy. Yeah, I will bring the red set with me for maybe changing into later? I am going to bring a little bit bigger of a purse so I can bring some supplies. I got some thigh high stockings (Yeehaw! I haven't had those in a long time).

You know, it's fun to get ready for the "liaison". I get to choose what I wear. I bet I even get to choose what to do (to a certain extent) during.[239] Hmmm, I wonder what the new guy would think if he knew I was writing about him.

---

[237] I don't even know where that nightie is. There was a set of pajamas in a plastic bag with that nightie and it's gone. Oh, well. I was saving it for some reason but it doesn't matter anymore.

[238] Planning the rendezvous.

[239] Nope, he took control and was a dick. I don't like him. It was a mistake.

Oh, my boss knows I am writing a book. I better not ever mention it again at work. They will forget and then it won't get mentioned. I still feel sad about Andre at times but it won't work out.[240] I think sometimes that maybe that when the resurrection comes, that I can meet him again and we can be together then because that is the ideal situation.[241] I don't know. Talk about wishing for the craziest things to happen but as they say, you never know. It could happen.[242]

Oh, and speaking of crazy, my ex-husband text me about some planet that is supposed to mess up the earth somehow (fly too close, hit the earth, I don't know. I didn't read the stuff on the internet). And he wanted to speak with me and his other ex about a contingency plan to save his two sons (one is Nathan). I did not even reply to that text. I just laughed because it just sounded insane. Yeah, right. Without no women, the human-race isn't being saved. Anyway, I wrote more but it was just crap so I deleted it. I'm tired. Goodnight.

Sunday morning

You know, I don't think there has been a day that has gone by since I came back from Tucson that I haven't cried at one point. Yes, I already cried this morning. It was that I bought a couple of nighties to wear for the new guy (yes, I couldn't bring myself to wear the one I wore for Andre) and I was disappointed that Andre won't ever see me in them. I also fantasied about the new guy and going to a comic-con with him. So, then I thought I wanted to go with Andre. And I cried. Again. This is so weird.

---

[240] Slowly descending back to earth.

[241] I don't want to be with him anymore. I like my new (current) guy better. Much better.

[242] Wishful thinking, for sure.

I wonder why this is happening to me. I know why. Because I thought I would be a big girl and hire myself a man to keep me company (and possibly have sex with). It was all just going to be fun. And wow, it was. But the aftermath was nothing I expected. But who could expect this? Quick summary. Went to Tucson. Saw a concert. Spent time with an Escort. Connected on a deep level with said escort. We part because different worlds. New guy pops up[243]. And the story goes on.

Oh, does it ever!!! I got curious and I looked at Andre's "The Most Popular Social Media" page. So, I saw a comment on a photo that he posted and it was from his ex. So, click the link. I scroll through a lot of stuff but on Jan 10th, there is a photo of her, Andre and a few others. And "a couples" photo. I got a uneasy feeling. I am a glutton for punishment, I guess. But I now know that I won't ever see him again. Ever. It's really time to let go. Really let go. I am not a fool. But I feel like one. Man, this sucks. But it's my own fault. But would I rather be ignorant? Not really.

Ok, on with sex with the new guy. And I might as well wash that nightie. Hahahahaha. Ahh, I knew it was over. It's ok (but really, I am sad). But why am I sad? Do I think I will never meet another guy like him?

At least I gave him the most wonderful goodbye email. I almost emailed him again. Oh, that would have been so bad. I wrote out that I found out, then I typed out that I thank him for what he did for me and then I asked for no reply. I started editing it and then I realized that I really don't have anything to say so I deleted it. Whew, avoided another bullet.

What do I really want to say? He did tell me he didn't have time

---

[243] Not the man I am seeing "now". The guy I was using to forget Andre with.

for me. He left out the part because he is trying to get back with his ex. But they were together for 3 years. I hope I helped him with whatever he needed at the time. That's all it was for. At least I have these great memories. I must leave them at that. Ahh, heart breaking again. I just can't wait for this to be over. It will be. It will be. The 11th can't be soon enough.[244]

A Day Later?

Oh, I am a fool. Such a fool. He was with her on Christmas.[245] And he texted me. Oh, I am bad. I am so bad. I am an idiot. Such an idiot. Oh, I shouldn't beat myself up. I am trying hard not to. But man, I am dumb, dumb, dumb. Oh, God. I am dumb. I should have done this earlier. Well, I am not a priority. So, here it goes. Fuck Andre!!!!!!!!!!! Yay, it's the moment I have been waiting for, for so long. Fuck, FUCK, FUCK, FUCK!!!!!!!!!!!!!!!!!!!!

So much anger. Breathe. Breathe. Ok, better now (that was only 20 seconds – tops).

I will never tell anyone because I feel like a fool.[246] Maybe I won't change the names to protect the NOT SO INNOCENT!!!!!!!!!!!! Ok, I will change the name but I am not changing the events. He does not deserve that. He was nice to me but I was so naive. Wow, this is just ridiculous. My emotions got the better of me. He must think I am a fool. I should tell him. Nah. Wow, that was a lesson. What a lesson. Just yesterday, I was asking God what lesson I am supposed

---

[244] That date came and went because the fling never contacted me. I wish I never met up with him but oh, well. All these lessons were learned.

[245] I found out by clicking on "The Most Popular Social Media". If you want to keep a secret, don't put it there. The whole world can see.

[246] Except I will write a book about it.

to learn from this. Now I know. Now I need to rethink my liaison. Oh, no! I need time.

I hope that everyone who reads this learns from my mistake. Was it a mistake? The event wasn't but the aftermath was. Man, I feel stupid. I don't even want to admit this stuff. Ugh!!!!!!

I don't think he lied. But maybe he did. Boy, that was an elaborate lie, if it was. Like I said, I need time. I finally got the text in PDF form so I guess it's time to delete him from my phone.[247] I will save it in multiple places before I do. Like I said, It's history. It all happened. Going to walk the dog.

So, back from walking the dog. Now that I have had time to think, I have no right to be angry. I got what I paid for. Little did I know my emotions would drive me crazy. Yes, we had that connection but that doesn't matter anymore. He let me go at the appropriate time and I learned things at the appropriate time.

All things happen so I can grow and move on. And I am moving on. I was thinking about changing my vacation, but I shouldn't. Haha. It's an evil reason why I won't. In case he calls, because he knows I will be there, I will get the joy of saying no to him. I don't think it will be hard at this point.

Whew. It finally happened. I am over him. It took a lot. And I will still think of him but I will now remember we have our own separate lives.[248] I mattered at the moment but not anymore. And that is how he should be. He did change me for the better. And he won't benefit. And I say that with pride now.

Ahh, he was a great guy. I hope he doesn't forget me. But if he

---

[247] I found out that the app I used didn't really copy all of the texts so I had to manually get them out of the phone.

[248] Nope, I won't. I don't think of him at all. He doesn't matter. It's all in the past.

does, does it matter? Not anymore. I won't hear from him again and I am so lucky about that. I must get those texts from my phone. I didn't get everything I need. Once I do that, I will delete him from my phone. I won't be journaling so much because I must concentrate on that. I got to get him gone.

I am embarrassed about some of the things I wrote earlier in this book. Really embarrassed. Man, I thought it was going to be hard to edit before. Now it's going to be truly painful. I am going to go through it because my goal is to write a book and I have always wanted to. When I was a child I did have a very short story printed in the San Mateo Times. But I had to wait to finally have a subject worth writing about. This is the story worth telling.

I guess the original title stands. I was thinking of changing it because it was negative but there are lots of negatives going on. There were lots of positives, too.

I should think about things. I am tired. Sometimes when I start thinking, I feel like a fool and I must talk myself back to reality. It's not my fault. I don't think he meant to lead me on.[249] Maybe he did because three times I said goodbye and he dragged me back in. He should have not contacted me ever, after that afternoon. Oh, well. Like I said, I need to get a clear head. I will be back much later.

---

[249] It's so hard to know what to think so I just don't think about it anymore.

THE REALIZATION

I T'S 3:12 AM Monday Morning. I am doing the final entry for "Andre". I am so done. So, so done.[250] I spent so much energy, emotions and time, on what? Nothing. Man, I realize now that I was a fool but I really couldn't help myself[251]. It really was a strange experience but I have decided to put it all behind me.

I do have final thoughts, as I always do. First, I am so happy to be closing this chapter of my life. It really did drain me mentally and physically. I lost 10 pounds. All foolish things I did for "love". I don't even think I love him (anymore?).[252]

Well, when you get taken a fool, things change. It's funny, timing is everything. It seemed, that at the end here, I learned exactly what I needed at the right time. I wonder why he kept hanging on. Maybe he just wanted to keep his options open. There are a lot of things I don't know and will never know. And that's ok.

---

[250] Very tired sigh.

[251] I really couldn't. I think about it now and I have a hard time believing it happened.

[252] Ever? Was it chemicals in my brain? That's all I can think it was because I am not that way. I don't understand why I was like that, back then.

I have learned many things about myself and life. I never, ever want to go through that again. I know that when I go through and edit this, there will be red flags galore.[253] But I didn't and couldn't see them. I wonder why? Are emotions that strong? Well, I did compare it to quitting cocaine. I wonder if down the line I will regret my decision for Tucson.

What makes this bad is, that originally, I thought he was sincere (he told me so) and now I have doubts. Or maybe he was just confused. In the end, he did the right thing by telling me he didn't have time for me (but he would if I paid for it).[254] I knew that he didn't want to make time for me. And I know why. I feel jaded so my feelings of good wishes for him have diminished.

My goodbye email is what I should have followed (advice-wise). I wrote it and it's true, if anything. One day, when I look back, I wonder what I will think. Editing time will do that.

Back to Andre. All the tears are done. I am not putting any more energy into this. The high at the beginning was so strong. I went crazy.

RED FLAGS!!!!!!!! JUST THINKING BACK, SO, SO MANY. I won't beat myself up for them. I will just learn. Oh, I better laugh about this because if I don't, I will cry. I was naive. How can I be naïve at this age? Boy, was I ever! But I know if I was outside, looking in, it would have been seen, all the red flags. Oh, well. Is there anything else to say?

I am not coming back to this section to add new material. The

---

[253] And so much pain and embarrassment. I am almost done editing but I skipped over one part. You know what part it was. I never read it.
[254] Figures.

only way he will get more page time is if he contacts me again[255] but I sure do hope not. I would have to tell him the truth and I don't want to do that.

Of course, I am putting it all out there for the world to see. I think I will make the location the North Pole and I went to see the Beatles. That will protect the innocents. And I will do that.

He never did say anything bad to me. Behind the scenes, not so good. And that article I found about him might have been true. See, because he hid things, I don't trust him. And he said he was honest with me. Does leaving things out considered to be honesty? I don't think so. Ahh, I always wondered who took those photos he posted on "The Most Popular Social Media."

Nothing changed with this new information as far as status goes. I am just more enlightened now. I realized that my mind was my own worst enemy. Would I want to go through it again? No way. Never, ever. Lesson learned.

Goodbye Andre. This time for good. I do believe our time together was honest. Just all the crap afterwards was just that, crap. I knew one day it would come to this. You were no good for me. I hope one day I can look fondly at our time together (because in some ways you were good for me). I really would like to. Time will tell. I can't say goodbye mean because it's not in my nature. So, Goodbye Andre. Thank you for all the valuable lessons. I wouldn't have learned them without you.

I hung on two weeks longer than I should have. My goodbye email was the end and I knew it but I always had a little hope in my back pocket but the pocket has ripped and it all blew away in the wind.

---

[255] During my vacation.

I knew what was happening most of the time but I couldn't help myself, so I forgive myself. Last tears, for myself, for being a fool.

Many Weeks Later

From my Phone Screen:
271 messages will be deleted
Cancel - Delete
Deleted

He is gone. It took me so long to get rid of him (in text form) in my phone. Five Whole Months! For a long time, I just couldn't go back and read the texts. It was too painful. I know now I was just a fool. But I am also a very nice person so I was doing what I thought would be the right thing to do at the time. I try to be kind. I wish my emotions hadn't gotten the best of me.

But I did learn so much. Not necessarily from him but from the fallout. If I don't know something, I will research it until I learn what is going on.

In that process, I learned about myself and who I really am. That is how I turned out to be this amazing, confident woman.

I am now self-assured. I won't put up with any BS anymore. If a man doesn't want to be with me, that is his loss. I know I am a great person and I have lots to give. I am also very sexy. I love sex and I love performing in the bedroom. I am alive. Any man would be lucky to have me.

Would I want to go through this again? I am not sure I would want to but at least I don't have that option. What happened, happened and for me it turned out great. For Andre? Who knows?

I never saw him in Santa Barbara and basically, he is just a memory. A memory I will never forget. The good and the bad.

And this chapter of my life ends. I am off to the next adventure!!!

The End

Printed in the United States
By Bookmasters